# HANGROPE HERITAGE

# HANGROPE HERITAGE

## TOM WEST

**THORNDIKE**
**CHIVERS**

This Large Print edition is published by Thorndike Press, Waterville, Maine, USA
and by BBC Audiobooks Ltd, Bath, England.

Thorndike Press is an imprint of The Gale Group.

Thorndike is a trademark and used herein under license.

The text of this Large Print edition is unabridged.

Other aspects of the book may vary from the original edition.

Set in 16 pt. Plantin.

**LIBRARY OF CONGRESS CATALOGING-IN-PUBLICATION DATA**

West, Tom, 1895–
   Hangrope heritage / by Tom West.
     p. cm. — (Thorndike Press large print western)
   ISBN-13: 978-0-7862-9955-3 (lg. print : alk. paper)
   ISBN-10: 0-7862-9955-X (lg. print : alk. paper)
   1. Large type books. I. Title.
PS3545.E8336H36 2007
813'.54—dc22
                                             2007030751

BRITISH LIBRARY CATALOGUING-IN-PUBLICATION DATA AVAILABLE

Published in 2007 in the U.S. by arrangement with
Golden West Literary Agency.
Published in 2008 in the U.K. by arrangement with
The Golden West Literary Agency.

U.K. Hardcover: 978 1 405 64350 4 (Chivers Large Print)
U.K. Softcover: 978 1 405 64351 1 (Camden Large Print)

Printed in the United States of America on permanent paper
10 9 8 7 6 5 4 3 2 1

# Hangrope Heritage

# I

When Circle B hands strung up old Jake Harper back in the Aridos Hills for rustling six prime steers, it was generally agreed that the old soak got what was coming.

In the opinion of Big Basin folks, Jake had never amounted to a barrel of shucks. So the incident was promptly forgotten.

But for a chance newspaper item, his bones might have crumbled into dust before word of his demise percolated outside the Basin.

As it was, less than a month after he strangled on a rope, Dan Harper, one of Jake's three sons, came upon the item in a frayed issue of *The Bonita County Bulletin*. Which was why Jake's boys were now gathered in a room of the Stockyards Hotel, El Paso.

Brow furrowed, Pat Harper paced the threadbare carpet of the boxy hotel room, perusing the yellowed newspaper clipping.

It was terse and to the point:

## JAKE HARPER HANGED

Jake Harper, an oldtimer in Big Basin, was summarily hanged by irate cattlemen on Thursday last. Rustlers have long been taking a heavy toll of Basin herds and Harper had long been suspect. A bunch of Circle B two-year-olds, their brands freshly doctored, provided the evidence that cut short the rustler's brand-blotching career. The steers were found penned in a box canyon nearby Harper's hard-scrabble hill ranch.

Watching him, the bearded Dan perched on the bed while Tom hunkered by the door, chewing a quirley. The three were plainly brothers, cast from a common mold, with the same rugged features, pitch-black eyes, stubborn jawlines. Pat, although the youngest — scarce in his twenties — was the most prosperous and partner in a profitable horse ranch. Tom held down a cattle-punching job, and Dan was a stage driver.

"Wal?" drawled Dan, as Pat crushed the creased piece of newsprint in a rope-wealed fist.

"You surprised?" said Pat. "Paw always

did fancy a steak off another man's steer."

The youngest of the Harpers was not tall, but broad in the shoulder, tough as a range colt. Short, black hair, too crisp for the comb, curled above sunbrowned features scraped razor smooth. He wore the plaid shirt and loose hanging vest of the range, and a faded red bandanna was knotted around his neck. The walnut butt of a .45 protruded from the holster slung around his waist and his eyes held a lurking belligerence.

Tom laughed wryly. "You hit the bull's-eye," he acknowledged. "Reckon the old pelican just got a mite too ambitious."

The bed creaked protest as the bearded Dan stirred impatiently. "I've got different ideas," he growled. "Sure the Old Man may have butchered a stray steer occasional, but he was never no hog. I just can't figure him running off a passel of Circle stock. The old coot never had that amount of ambition. I got a hunch he was framed."

"Why in heck would he be framed?" demanded Pat with plain disbelief.

Dan raised his shoulders. "Your guess is as good as mine, kid. I been hearing stories about Basin rustling. It's bad! Couldbe a gang's at work, and couldbe they planted them steers to muddy the trail."

9

"Hogwash!" interjected Pat.

"And I reckon we should look into it," continued Dan, blandly ignoring the interruption.

"See here, Dan," said the younger man. "I got a partner waiting up at Amarillo, and a slew of broncs to break. What's more, I got to fill an Army contract for remounts. You figure I can find time to play detective around Big Basin?"

"It couldn't be that you lack sand?" drawled the bearded man, surveying him coolly.

Pat tautened, fingering the butt of his gun. "What do you figure?" he challenged.

Tom straightened hastily and thrust between them. "For gosh sakes! Quit climbing each other's humps." He eyed the eldest. "There's no call to prod, Dan!"

"I still claim," persisted the stage driver, "that we should poke into this. The Old Man might have had no ambition beyond swilling rotgut and lying around like a hound in the sun, but he was our paw. If the old horntoad was framed, something's got to be done about it." Jaw pugnacious, he met the gaze of the two younger men.

Pat nodded in reluctant agreement.

"Sure, sure!" agreed Tom hastily. "What you figure to do, Dan?"

The bearded man said nothing, just slapped his holstered gun. As the two stood waiting, he fished out a deck of dog-eared cards.

"Shuffle!" he told Pat laconically, and held out the deck.

Unsmiling, the youngest man took the pack, shuffled, passed the cards back.

"Now," explained his elder brother, "we cut. Gent who turns up low card hits for Big Basin, pokes around and maybe takes action." He eyed the sober-faced Pat. "Suit you?"

Pat shrugged resignedly. Ever since they were buttons, he thought, Dan had bossed him and Tom. He was still boss.

"Ace's high!" reminded Dan, and extended the deck to Tom. The puncher cut — jack of spades. Pat reached and exposed the deuce of diamonds. Dan divided the deck last — three of spades.

"Guess you're elected, kid!" he told Pat coolly and came to his feet. He laid a hand on the youngest Harper's broad back. "You head into trouble, send word — we'll come arunning."

"Reckon I can kill my own skunks," returned Pat stiffly, "providing there's any around — which I doubt."

"I can sniff 'em right now," grunted Dan.

11

Forking a claybank, bedroll bulking behind the cantle, Pat Harper followed the stage road that wound across the desolate expanse east of El Paso. Behind him, mountains bulked blue against the horizon and the towering spur of El Capitan was etched in sharp profile.

The young horse breaker was in no good humor. The contract which he and Hoot Fuller, his partner, held for Army remounts had a time limit. Without interruption, he and Hoot had a bellyful of work ahead. Now odds were that the contract would be blown sky-high.

Trouble was, he considered irately, this trip to Big Basin was plain waste. Damn Dan and his hunches! Paw had tangled his spurs and got his comeuppance. There was nothing could be done about it now. A noose had been the time-honored penalty for rustling as long as he could remember, and it seemed the Old Man had just played out of luck, or maybe old age had made him careless.

The Harpers in Big Basin had always stunk. Their mother had died so far back that she was no more than a faint memory.

They had run wild on the hard-scrabble holding back in the Aridos Hills. If there was any deviltry afoot, Pat reflected, the Harper boys were someway involved. Jake, their father, never had more ambition than a hog in a wallow — not after their mother passed away. All he ever craved was to set around and soak up redeye.

No cowman in the Basin would hire a Harper, so when Dan reached an age when he could hold down a job, he just naturally drifted out of Big Basin; which went for Tom and finally himself.

So the Old Man was eventually left on the moldering spread with the coyotes for company. Not that loneliness ever bothered Jake. Paw never craved company and never lacked for meat — which went for hootch, too. Since he couldn't read or write and the boys never had a yen to return to their old stamping ground, they'd lost sight of the Old Man through the years. If Dan hadn't lit on that newspaper item, likely Jake's bones would have bleached before they wised up to his fate.

Well, cogitated the rider, if Bones Bailey, the deputy in Adobe Wells, was still on the job, he'd get the lowdown on the lynching pronto and maybe pull out for Amarillo within the week. With luck, he and Hoot could still deliver under that Army contract.

It was just too bad about Paw, but what was it he'd once heard a preacher say — a man reaped what he sowed. The Old Man had been too doggoned slothful to do much sowing, but it was a sure thing he'd scattered a few wild oats.

# II

Adobe Wells hadn't changed a mite in six years, reflected Pat, as the claybank jogged between two rows of rock-and-adobe structures spaced unevenly along the broad stretch of Main Street. From their fronts, wooden canopies projected over shady plankwalks. It was close upon noon and the town drowsed, torpidly enduring the heat. Straw-hatted hombres slacked in spots of shade; a scattering of saddle horses stood droop-hipped outside The Wagon Wheel Saloon; a buckboard was drawn up outside Shrader's rambling general store, two broncs in the traces.

Then the rider chuckled at sight of a form hunched on a bench outside a yellowing adobe which carried a faded sign: *Deputy Sheriff.* The object of his attention was a long-gaited, bony individual, dehydrated by the desert sun. A metal badge glinting on his gray shirt, he sat stiff and unmoving as a

15

cigar store Indian.

Old Bones Bailey, deputy sheriff, was as unchangeable as the town, thought Pat. When he'd last glimpsed the lawman six years back, he'd been hunched exactly in the same manner, in the same spot. Perched on the bench, he seemed to be dozing, but, like a questing hawk, Bones never missed anything and that long-barreled Colt he packed was as deadly as a striking rattler.

The rider reined to the hitchrail in front of Bones, swung out of leather and stood beating the dust off his shirt and pants. The deputy watched him, still as a graven image.

"Howdy, Bones!" greeted Pat, ducking under the rail.

The lawman's head jerked in curt recognition. Pat dropped down on the bench beside him, yanked out the makin's and began to build a cigarette. " 'Member me?" he asked.

"Ain't likely to forget no high-stepping Harper," snapped the deputy. He nodded at the dust-coated claybank. "Prime piece of horseflesh!"

"I raise 'em."

"You Harpers never raised nothing but hell in the Basin." But the Harper boys, mused the old deputy to himself, were never vicious, just full of devilment. Pat was the

16

only one who showed any stability. He stuck to school while his two elder brothers quit and spent their time hunting and harassing the citizenry. What was more, he never shied away from work — mucked in the Adobe Livery to acquire sufficient dinero to buy a good saddle and rigging for his old cow pony. Sure different from old Jake. The hardest work Jake ever did was ride out of the hills when his supply of hootch ran low, slouched on his old applehorn saddle, to stock up again at The Wagon Wheel.

Pat's voice interrupted his cogitations. "Reckon we were kinda wild," he admitted. "Wal, we're broke to harness now."

"I wouldn't gamble on it," rasped Bones. His head swiveled and his flinty eyes focused the visitor. "So the hanging pulled you back!"

"How did you guess?"

"Knowing the Harpers, I figured one of you boys would bob up, itching to even things up."

"You got me wrong, Bones," the other assured him earnestly. "Maybe Paw got what was coming, but Dan's nursing a notion the Old Man didn't get a fair shake. I was elected to check."

"The Circle boys made no mistake," returned the deputy harshly. "Rustlers been draining the Basin. Folks kinda wondered howcome the old buzzard got by without working a lick. Wal, they located them Circle steers not half a mile from his hangout, corraled in a canyon. Every brand had been worked into a Hobbled H."

"Heck, that's no proof Paw ran 'em off!"

Unheeding, the deputy continued. "They uncovered two more Circle B hides moldering in a corner of Jake's barn, and a third rotting in the brush." He spat. "Jake lived on Circle beef for years."

Bones probably hit the bull's-eye there, considered Pat, but one beef would supply all the meat the Old Man could eat in months. Aloud, he asked, "What did Paw have to say about it?"

"Hell, he was too drunk to argue. Even if he'd been cold sober, the Circle boys were too hot and bothered to listen."

"Who bossed the necktie party — Bull Bradley?"

The deputy fished a corncob pipe out of a vest pocket, slowly stuffed the blackened bowl from a sack of twist. "Wal," he returned slowly, "officially, I don't know a durned thing about the showdown. Lynching ain't exactly legal. Howsoever, it's customary where brand-blotchers are concerned. The story is that Matt presided."

18

It would be Matt Bradley! The Bradleys and Harpers had been feuding ever since the Harper wagon first rolled into the Aridos Hills, his maw sitting beside Paw on the driver's seat and three buttons peering over the endgate. In those days the Old Man had been full of sap. He'd built a house, a clapboard barn and a corral, wire-fenced a pasture and acquired a bunch of yearlings. Then, like a brush fire, the pox had swept through Big Basin. Maw was dead within the week. After that, Paw fell apart, lost all ambition, craved nothing but the bottle.

Craggy-featured Bull Bradley rodded the Circle B, the biggest spread in the Basin, and his range flowed into the hills. Although graze was poor in the parched *malpais* and his beef seldom strayed up from the vast Basin flats, he'd never stomached the Harpers. To him they were squatters and pests. Even his two redheaded kids, Matt and Diane, carried the hate. They met up with the Harper boys in the schoolhouse at Adobe Wells. Since Dan and Tom played hookey most of the time, he bore the brunt. Matt was four or five years older, bigger, tougher. Diane was a pig-tailed, slim-legged wildcat. Whenever the pair ganged up on him, which was often, he rode home so bruised and battered he could scarce sit the saddle. Paw never cared a damn, but Dan finally took it up. He'd beaten the daylights out of the Circle heir and thereafter the belligerent Matt had shied away from the Harper boys. So, reflected Pat, Matt had finally collected for that beating. With a start, he realized that the deputy's deepset eyes focused him.

"Matt got a long memory," drawled Bones.

*The old horned toad must be a mind reader,* reflected Pat. He grinned self-consciously. "Guess so," he admitted.

The deputy straightened his long, gawky form. "I sassayed out and collected Jake's belongings," he said. "Them that was worthwhile. Reckon I'll hand 'em over."

Pat dogged him into the adobe, which served as the deputy's living quarters as well as office. The deputy hefted a bulky gunnysack from behind his stove. With the sweep of an arm he cleared half a table of its clutter and emptied the contents of the gunnysack upon it.

A motley array spilled out — lindsey shirts, pants, loose shells, a jackknife, a photo of a young man and woman standing stiffly, a worn, black-bound bible. Almost reverently, Pat reached for the bible.

"That was Maw's," he volunteered. He flicked up the cover. On the flyleaf, inscribed

20

in a cramped angular hand, were the birth-dates of himself and his brothers.

The deputy lifted an old Springfield rifle off a shelf and added it to the pile, fished a buckskin pouch out of a can and dropped it into Pat's palm. "Five hundred dollars — even," he said. "Wal, I guess that's the tally."

Pat stared. "You say five hundred dollars?" he questioned.

"Fifty gold eagles," said Bones. "Surprised?"

Pat nodded mutely.

"Kind of cinches things, don't it?"

Without replying, Pat returned the gold to the pouch and dropped it into a pocket. Then, as the deputy watched silently, he began stuffing his dead father's possessions back into the gunnysack.

Neither spoke as he shouldered the gunny-sack and packed it outside. The old deputy sauntered out as he secured it beside the bedroll behind the cantle.

"Guess the old moseyhorn had to live," said Bones.

"Not that way!" returned Pat shortly. He set a foot in the stirrup, swung into leather, raised an arm in farewell.

Pondering, he jogged south, heading out of town the way he had entered. For the first time the full impact of his father's crime hit him. Althought the newspaper story had pointed to the Old Man's guilt, he had unconsciously nursed a hope that Jake was innocent — until Bones had dumped that pouch containing $500 gold in his hand. That cinched it, as the deputy said. There was nothing he could do now except ride back to El Paso and break the news to Dan.

Maybe, he mused, if he hadn't been so eager to gather dinero himself and prove to the world that a Harper could amount to something worthwhile, he would have kept in touch with the Old Man and straightened him out.

Well, it was too late now. Always, he'd have that ghost lurking back of his mind — an old man, drunk, a proven rustler, hanging from a branch, surrounded by derisive punchers — his father!

A yell from behind stirred him from his abstraction and jerked his head around. Bones, his long legs pumping, was racing across street toward the ponies tied outside the saloon. Men were darting out of store doorways. And racing toward him, enveloped in thick-rising dust — eyes white-rimmed, necks outstretched, hoofs pounding in a frenzied tattoo — were the two broncs he had seen tied to the buckboard outside Shrader's store. Behind them, the buckboard swayed crazily, wheels spinning, jolting from pothole to pothole, threatening to crash at any moment. As the runaways whirled past, he caught a glimpse of a girl, thick copper hair streaming, red lips a tight slash against pale features, bouncing on the driver's seat, futilely tugging at the lines as she strove to check the runaways.

# III

As rising dust blocked out the hurtling buckboard, Pat raised his reins and roweled. The claybank's hooves sprayed dirt as it leapt forward. In seconds, the pony was pounding through hovering dust in the wake of the runaways.

Speedily, Main Street dropped behind. The pursuing rider found himself racing across a rolling plain that stretched, like an earthy sea, into the veiling purple of distance. He saw that the runaways, from habit, were following the deep-rutted tracks of a stage road that snaked across the flats. If those crazed broncs took a notion to cut off at an angle across the swales, that buckboard jouncing wildly behind them would overturn for sure and the girl would be out of luck.

Urging the claybank with voice and rowel, he steadily pulled closer to the whirling vehicle. Wind whistling through its nostrils, his lathered pony drew abreast of the jolting buckboard.

He glimpsed the girl, a gray ghost through a fog of fast-rising dust, still frantically sawing on the lines, so intent on checking the team that he doubted if she were aware of his presence. Slowly, the claybank forged ahead, drew level with the broncs' drumming hooves, pulled up to their outstretched heads. He neckreined his mount over, reached out and grabbed the bit chain of the nearer runaway, began curbing his own pony.

Gradually, the crazed broncs slowed. Finally, he brought them to a halt, chests heaving like bellows, coats sweat-plastered.

Lines limp in her hands, the girl sat slack upon the seat. *Pretty as a heart flush,* he registered. The tangle of rich, burnished hair framed flawless features. Full breasts swelled beneath a white shirtwaist, now tinged gray with dust.

The girl's small chin had a stubborn angle and her red lips were firm. Despite the strain of the turbulent ride, with death hovering at her elbow, her glance, as she focused Pat with vivid green eyes, was cool and speculative. And, when she spoke, her voice was without a quaver.

"Well," she said, "they spooked!"

"And 'most piled your rig."

She shrugged. "They would have run it out, but anyway, I'm sure thanking you, Mister —" her glanced quickened. "Say, you wouldn't be Pat Harper?"

He nodded and inquired, grinning, "And you wouldn't be that long-legged school gal with a hair-trigger temper tagged Diane Bradley?"

"I certainly am!" At a thought, both her hands went to the thick disorder of her hair. "I must look a fright!"

"You sure look good to me!" he assured her, and the tremor in his voice drew a quick glance from the girl. She jammed the gray Stetson dangling down her back upon her head and became busy thrusting unruly strands of hair beneath it.

"What brought you back to —" she inquired offhand, then abruptly checked. Her green eyes raised to meet his again. "Oh, the hanging!"

"Yep!" he replied tonelessly. "The hanging! I guess the Old Man tangled his spurs and Matt strung him up."

"Don't blame Matt!" she begged. "I know he's headstrong, but you know how folks feel about rustlers. Dad's worried stiff over our losses. He told Matt to turn your father over to the law, but the men got out of hand."

"I guess that didn't break Matt's heart," he threw back.

She shrugged helplessly. "Let's forget it, Pat! What's done can't be undone."

"To a Bradley," he retorted, his tone icy, "the Harpers were always vermin, on a level with coyotes and skunks."

"That isn't so!" she protested hotly. "The families just — clashed, that's all!" Then the girl tautened, sudden unease in her green eyes. "You didn't come back to — to . . ."

"Call Matt out!" he broke in. "Heck, no! I just craved to get the lowdown on the hanging. Paw knew the penalty for swinging a wide loop. Guess I've got nothing against Matt."

"I'm so glad!" The girl's relief was plain. They eyed each other silently, Pat with an admiration he found difficult to conceal; the girl with curiosity and a certain bashfulness at the intent scrutiny of his dark eyes. Who would ever have figured that the stringy Bradley girl would have developed into this copper beauty!

A little breathlessly she questioned, "I suppose you've met May Matthews?"

Pat shook his head. "I met no one outside of old Bones. Who's May Matthews?"

"The daughter of that man with T.B.

They've been living up at the Harper place for several months."

"With Paw?" His tone was incredulous.

"Sure! I supposed they were friends, or tenants."

Pat pushed back his hat and ran fingers through his short, bristly hair. This didn't make good sense. For years the Old Man never craved any company except his own. He always shied away from strangers, and the Harpers sure had no relatives named Matthews.

"Never heard of 'em," he confessed.

The girl's glance raised beyond him. "Company's coming," she said.

He swung around in the saddle. A mile or more to the south, the huddle of buildings that was Adobe Wells botched the sunbaked plain. Between, dust plumed from the curving stage road, thrown up by a little troop racing toward them. Leading the pack was a horseman. Close behind him smoked a buggy and tailing the buggy were other riders. Pat smothered his disgust and mentally abandoned a half-formed plan to tie his pony behind the buckboard and drive the girl back to her father's ranch.

With no enthusiasm, he greeted Bones Bailey, as the gaunt deputy checked his blowing pony and stepped down. The buggy halted behind him and a short, jovial man emerged. He was garbed in a rumpled store suit and a black bag dangled from one hand. Pat recognized the local medico as Dr. Lockwood — healer and undertaker. Seemed the doctor had always been around Adobe Wells. As always, he needed a shave and likely still enjoyed a snort of bourbon and hand of poker. But at that he was the most valuable man in town.

The deputy stood lamping the two broncs, now standing hipshot, apparently half asleep. "Guess you won't be needed, doc," he threw over a shoulder as the medico bustled up.

The doctor paused beside the buckboard and stood looking up at the girl's composed features. "You all right, Diane?" he inquired.

"Never felt better!" she returned coldly. "Sorry to have made myself such a pest." She grasped the lines. "Well, I'll be moving along!"

"Say," put in Pat. "You sure you can handle them broncs?"

"Watch me!" she threw back carelessly and jerked the lines. The broncs threw their weight against the traces and trotted off at a lamblike pace, the buckboard rattling behind them.

"It takes more'n a runaway to rouse a

Bradley," grunted Bones. He strode to his pony. Pat and the doctor stood watching the buckboard as it moved away, bumping along the uneven trail.

"There's one thing that girl doesn't lack," murmured Lockwood, "— spunk!" He turned to Pat. "Too bad about your father!"

Pat raised his shoulders, mind on Diane Bradley.

"Of course," continued the doctor, "the old fellow wouldn't have lasted long anyway."

Pat came out of his abstraction, eying the medico with quick inquiry. "Howcome?" he asked.

"Liver trouble, advanced stage. Then he was so crippled with rheumatism he could scarcely use his hands or sit a horse. He struggled to town to consult me less than a week before his — death. How he rode in, I'll never know. I drove him back to the hills in my buggy. Well, I can't afford to stand around yakking!" With a wave of the hand, the rotund doctor trotted back to his buggy.

Pat sat the saddle, watching him wheel his plump mare and spin off. But his mind was not on the doctor, but on his father. How in creation, he wondered, could the Old Man round up and corral a bunch of wild steers, heat an iron and change their brands if he was so crippled by rheumatism he could scarce sit a horse? No one but an active man could have chased that stock up into the hills, and the branding chore would be tough for any one man to handle. Yet from what other source could he have obtained five hundred dollars — gold?

And this Matthews couple, living at the old place. Who were they? Dan and Tom would ask questions. Now he was in Big Basin he'd be crazy to return before he investigated. He raised his reins, heading back to town. Maybe he should stay over for a couple of days, book a room at the Adobe Hotel. At sunup he could hit for the Aridos Hills and check.

The sun rimmed the rugged outline of distant mountains and its rays — long, vague fingers of light — groped across the Basin, erasing the chill of night. Less than a few minutes, Pat figured, should see him at the hill ranch. He could be back and on the trail for El Paso before long.

Nodding as it labored upward, the clay-bank rounded the shoulder of a hill and a small clutter of buildings, weathered to a weary gray, came into view. Pat drew rein, assailed by a flood of long-buried memories.

This was the only home he had ever remembered.

His survey took in a squat adobe, a roofed gallery built along its front. Nearby were a barn and a square, clapboard shack. There was a small corral and a rectangle of wire-fenced pasture. Behind the adobe, chaparral made a verdant patch against the sun-baked slopes. That would be the location of the spring, he considered. Like Adobe Wells, the place hadn't changed a mite. There didn't seem to be any signs of life, except for three ponies drifting around the pasture.

He raised his reins and drifted down into the bowl. Drawing close, he glimpsed the form of a man seated in the shade of the gallery.

When he pulled rein a dozen paces from the man, he saw that the stranger was methodically laying out cards in three straight columns in what seemed to be a game of solitaire. So intent did he seem on the pasteboards that he was unaware of the visitor.

Pat sized him up. He was in his late thirties, the rider guessed, and looked like a city man, neatly garbed in clean white shirt, dark pants and moccasin slippers. His blond hair was neatly brushed back from a high forehead, and his sunken cheeks accentuated the angles of his sharp features. As Pat watched, he coughed and dabbed a handkerchief to his lips.

"Howdy!" hailed the rider.

The hollow-cheeked man looked up, nodded curtly and returned to his cards. Pat was fighting mounting irritation when the door of the adobe opened and a girl stepped out. This thorn had a rose, he thought, with quick interest. She was, he judged, barely in her twenties, tall and willowy. A neat blue-and-white calico dress displayed the curves of her slender form. Below a mass of curly dark brown hair, her features were finely cut, with wide-spaced gray eyes that reflected warmth and frankness. Her mouth was wide, generous, full lips parted in a welcoming smile.

Pat stepped down, ground-hitched the claybank and stepped forward, removing his hat. "The handle's Harper," he volunteered, "Pat Harper."

She looked him over in friendly approval. "Pat Harper!" she repeated. "Why, a Jake Harper lived here."

"He was my paw," he said shortly.

Her gray eyes telegraphed swift sympathy. "I'm so sorry about — what happened," she said, and her voice had a soothing, almost seductive quality that was pleasant to the ear. "Sit down — Pat!"

She gestured toward one of several rockers set around the gallery, then stepped to the well, dipped a mug of cool water and brought it to him as he sank into the rocker.

He drank gratefully, and set the empty mug aside. The girl drew up another rocker. "It's nice to have a visitor," she smiled. "Well, what brought you into these parched hills?"

"You!" he retorted. He softened the abruptness of the exclamation with a grin, adding, "I just couldn't figure Paw having boarders."

"Boarders!" Her laughter rang. "Why, my father bought this place. He paid poor old Jake Harper $500 — gold."

# IV

*Five hundred dollars — gold!* The import of the words struck Pat with the impact of a bullet. That explained the money in the buckskin pouch found by Bones Bailey — money which both he and the lawman had assumed was payment for rustled stock. To his mind, it was the only piece of concrete evidence against his father. The Circle steers could have been planted. The few rotting Circle hides uncovered around the place had likely been skinned off solitary beasts hazed into the hills through the years. The Harpers never denied themselves meat, not when a multitude of steers grazed across the stretches of the Basin below. To the rider's mind there was a vast difference between systematic rustling, and cutting out an occasional animal for meat.

The girl had come to her feet. "You'll want to look around," she said, "and revive memories. Let me show you where your father lived."

He followed her off the gallery as she led the way toward the clapboard shack. *So Paw had moved into the shack,* mused Pat. With his brothers, he had bunked there for years. The adobe only boasted two small rooms, with a lean-to kitchen in the rear. Paw had craved to be alone when he was drinking, which was most always.

When they were beyond earshot of the gallery, she turned, gray eyes seeking his. "What I really wanted to do," she confessed, "was apologize for Dad. Please don't be angry at his apparent discourtesy. I know he seems churlish, but he's sick, very sick, and he wants nothing but to be left alone."

"His T.B. bring you west?"

She nodded. "Dad was an accountant, a successful accountant, in Chicago. Doctors said a dry climate offered the only chance of checking the disease. So we exchanged the city for" — she spread her arms in a gesture of resignation — "this."

"It's kinda tough on you," he said.

"Don't women always have to serve — and suffer?" she replied quietly.

He thought of Diane Bradley, contrasting the copperhead with this gray-eyed, slender girl. Diane sure wouldn't subscribe to the doctrine of suffering and serving. Like all the Bradleys she craved the best, and grabbed it.

They sauntered past the shack, toward the pasture. May Matthews was the type of girl who made a man feel at ease. She made no demands, showed no resentment at being banished to this lonely spot, just imparted a soothing sense of companionship.

"Howcome you folks hit on this place, dumped back in the hills?" he inquired suddenly.

"Just accident," she returned wryly. "We came to Adobe Wells by train. More than anything else, Dad had an urge to get away from people. His disease embittered him. He heard of Jake Harper living back here alone and came out to see him. Apparently Jake was ailing, too." She smiled. "Everyone called Mr. Harper, Jake. Anyway, he agreed to sell cheap, provided he could continue to live in the shack, and I would prepare his meals." Dimpling, she concluded, "So I was elected chief cook and bottle washer, and here we are!"

"Wal, you sure brighten up the old homestead," he declared forcefully.

Side by side, they wandered around the wire-fenced pasture. "Ain't that Paw's buckskin?" inquired Pat, pausing and nodding toward a spur-scratched, saddle-galled old cow pony nosing the scant graze.

The girl nodded. "Mr. Bailey, the deputy, left the animal when he collected your father's belongings. He said it was a piece of crowbait, too aged and broken-winded to sell. So I suggested the poor creature be left here to end its days in peace."

"You would!" commented Pat fervently.

They moved on. Pat was in no hurry to break away and May Matthews seemed well content with his company. Odds were, he thought, any visitor made a welcome break in what must be to her an endless chain of days.

"Just what would you know about the hanging?" he asked, offhand.

The girl shivered, "Very little and that little I would like to forget. I was baking a cake when a number of cowboys suddenly invaded the place. I hurried outside and saw them drag poor Jake out of the shack, mount him upon a horse and race away with him. I was too scared to say or do anything."

"Paw make any protest?"

She hesitated. "He — drank, quite heavily."

"Too drunk to protest," commented Pat dryly.

She said nothing.

They had rounded the pasture and were

approaching the adobe again now. Pat checked by his pony. "Guess I'll amble along," he said. "It's sure been nice meeting you."

"You'll come again?" she questioned quickly, and he read warm appeal in her gray eyes.

"Sure will," he assured her emphatically. Then he, added, "If I stick around the Basin."

"Then you may leave?"

"I just wouldn't know," he returned slowly, and stepped into leather.

Engrossed in his card game, the hollow-checked man ignored as he shouted, "So long!"

Before dropping out of sight over the rim of the bowl, he checked his mount and turned in the saddle. Dwarfed by distance, a slim form stood by the gallery. He yanked off his Stetson, waved. A handkerchief fluttered in return. Then he drifted over the rise and the Harper place disappeared from view. It was a doggone crime, penning a nice gal like that back in these stark hills to minister to the wants of a surly recluse. Still, she'd uttered not one word of complaint, although it must have been hell tending to both a drunk and an invalid.

As his pony threaded through the chaos

39

of the Aridos Hills, dropping down into the Basin, he pondered on his father's hanging. Gone was the certainty that the Old Man had been guilty and had just happened to run out of luck. Jake had been framed to divert attention from the activities of a gang of rustlers, and also to salve the pride of Matt Bradley, Circle heir.

Bull Bradley, Matt's father, had never let up on the Harpers. From the time their wagon rolled into the hills he had plagued them. True the Harper boys paid off in kind, pestering the big Circle outfit by every means they could devise, from sticking burrs beneath the saddles of any Circle ponies they found tied on Main Street, to starting fires on Circle range, spooking Circle stock, slicing cinches.

Pat chuckled. They'd been hellions, but the domineering Bradley clan had asked for it. Dan had beaten the daylights out of Matt, too, when both boys were in their teens. Yep, the Harpers had held their end up, and the Bradleys never forgot or forgave. He guessed that Matt had nursed his hate, waited until the Old Man was left alone, practically helpless. Then the Circle scion had framed him with a bunch of stock. It must have been a cinch. Shadowed by the Harper reputation, Jake wouldn't have had a show. Likely, Big Basin said, "Good riddance!"

So that had been the reason for the uneasiness in Diane's eyes when she mentioned the hanging. She guessed; maybe she knew.

Unconsciously, the rider's jaw muscles hardened and his fists clenched. Mentally, he vowed that the murder would not go unavenged.

In Adobe Wells he held onto his room in the hotel. That evening found him with a foot on the rail in The Wagon Wheel, nursing a mug of beer. He'd decided to stick around and endeavor to nose out evidence that would clear his father of the rustling charge and tighten a noose around Matt Bradley's thick neck. The problem was just where to begin.

The saloon was a low-ceilinged rock-and-adobe structure. A long bar ran down one side. Two doorways had been punched in the rear wall, one gave admission to Ace Ackerman's — the proprietor's — office; the other to a small room where high-stake poker games were played. Brass oil lamps swung from the ceiling; small tables were scattered over the hard-packed dirt floor.

The sun had been down an hour and the batwings noised continuously on dusty hinges as men drifted in to belly up to the bar or drop down at a table.

Pat had been little more than a boy, going on sixteen, when he'd pulled out of the Basin. Punchers were a fiddle-footed breed. Men he had known by sight had drifted on; boys with whom he had sat in class were now men, changed beyond recognition. In point of fact, this was his first visit to the saloon. Compared to some of the glittering joints in El Paso, even in Amarillo, it was a dump, but the beer tasted just as good.

Gazing idly into the backbar mirror, he glimpsed two men pushing through the batwings, and tautened. The first was a broad shouldered rider, still young, coppery hair showing beneath the brim of his Stetson. He wore range garb, but its quality told that he was no thirty-and-found saddle stiff. His glove-fitting, handmade boots, reflected Pat, must have cost fifty dollars. The fancy Stetson probably had set him back another fifty, and his silk shirt was likely ticketed twenty-five dollars.

Plainly, his taste went to silver. The glossy metal was inlaid along his gunbelt; it decorated his holster and shone on the butt plates of his .45.

But it was the newcomer's features that drew Pat's attention like a magnet. Pale green eyes, hard and unfriendly, set above a straight, questing nose. His heavy jaw had an aggressive angle and his face was weathered, sunblasted. It all added up to give an impression of a domineering, reckless man.

Trailing him was a big, rawboned man, his mouth a thin slash against brown features, his eyes black, smoldering, watchful. He was lantern-jawed, with high cheekbones that hinted at a strain of Indian blood. His garb was more workman-like — gray shirt, waist Levis, a faded bandanna loose around his neck. The plain walnut butt of a gun protruding from a worn leather holster hinted that the weapon was intended more for service than show.

Pat turned to a puncher drinking beside him and inquired, "That Matt Bradley just came in?"

The other glanced briefly in the mirror. "Sure!" he replied.

"Who's the dusky gent tailing him?"

"Jules Garrott, Circle foreman."

Matt Bradley swaggered across the floor, considered Pat, as though he owned the saloon and everything in it. In Big Basin cattle meant power, and the Bradleys had power to spare.

He breasted the bar with his foreman just beyond Pat — only the puncher who had identified them between.

The apron promptly slid a bottle of bourbon and two glasses in their direction. Pat saw that Matt Bradley poured brim high; the foreman a scant two fingers. The Circle heir raised his glass to drink — and focused Pat's intent gaze in the backbar mirror.

"Gordamit, Jules," he bellowed. "No sooner do we clean out one coyote and one of his cubs bobs up."

His deep voice boomed through the saloon. The monotone of talk cut off abruptly, as though severed by a sharp knife. All heads swiveled.

Scenting trouble, the puncher beside Pat slid quietly away, so that no one stood between him and Matt Bradley. The Circle heir swung around to face him, green eyes derisive.

Pat's beer mug was still half full. He turned casually, the mug in his right hand. Deliberately, he flung its contents full into the heavy-jawed face.

# V

For an instant, Matt Bradley froze, stupified by surprise, the brown liquid streaking his face, draining off his chin, wetly patching his silk shirt. Then, with an enraged roar, he grabbed for the butt of his .45. Lips tight set, Pat stabbed for his own gun.

A short, compact man thrust between them. Ace Ackerman, gambler and proprietor of The Wagon Wheel, was a hatchet-faced rooster of a man with hard, smooth features, masked with a frozen smile of friendliness. His eyes were guarded, expressionless. Always he was garbed in sober black, and spotless white linen, his dark hair carefully slicked back. Few men made trouble with Ace; he packed too potent a sting in the form of a stubby Remington .41 — a conventional gambler's gun — small enough to nestle inconspicuously beneath his left armpit and deadly enough to fill a space in boothill. Pushed, he was apt to use it.

"Gentlemen!" he purred, right hand sliding beneath his dark coat. "No shooting in this saloon — please!"

"I don't need a gun. I'll tear the bustard apart with my hands," spluttered Bradley. He slipped the buckle of his gunbelt, swung it off. Garrott, beside him, caught the heavy belt, stood with it dangling from one hand.

Pat unbuckled his own gunbelt, dropped it on the bar, plunked his hat beside it.

A tenseness held the saloon. Though few were acquainted with Pat Harper, the hanging of his father was common knowledge, and patrons sensed a slap-bang dogfight was at hand. Neither Bull nor his son were overly popular around the Basin — they had gored too many of the smaller ranchers. Interest was high as to how this tough looking young stranger would acquit himself. It would be a sight for sore eyes to see a Bradley get his comeuppance.

Tables and chairs scraped as they were hastily pushed back to clear a space around the pair. Silently, patrons gathered around in a loose ring, tight anticipation on their faces.

Matt Bradley was plainly the older of the two, and he held the advantage of weight and size. But where his smaller opponent was all bone and muscle, the bigger man was fleshy, too fleshy. It was as though a leathery range colt were balking a sleek stallion.

Bradley launched the attack with a swift kick at his opponent's groin. Had it connected, the fight would have terminated right there. Pat, however, jerked backward, grabbed the swinging, sharp-toed riding boot with both hands and heaved. Unbalanced, Matt thudded down heavily on his back. Pat dropped the leg and jumped for the prostrate form. His boots slammed into Bradley's ribs. There are no Marquis of Queensbury's rules in a saloon fight. A bottle, the bottom knocked off, or the leg of a chair hastily yanked apart, were prize weapons.

Bradley rolled, arms crossed over his face for protection. Blindly, as Pat followed him, boots flailing his torso, he grabbed for a chair, hurled it. Pat checked to fend off the missile; hard-breathing, the Circle scion scrambled to his feet. Bitter animosity glinting in his eyes, he rushed at the lighter man.

Crouched, chin tucked in, Pat met the assault, fists pumping. For awhile, there was no sound in the saloon save the dull, flat thud of knuckles upon flesh, the intake of Bradley's breath, and gasping grunts from

each as pounding fists sank home. Unnoticed by the absorbed spectators, a gaunt,
long-gaited individual, badge pinned to his
shirt, slid through the batwings and stood
back against the wall.

Pat's body quivered before a barrage of
blows. With silent ferocity, he fought back,
thrilled with bitter joy as he felt the other's
body quiver before the impact of his
bunched fists. A fiery shower of sparks
cascaded as a hard fist crashed into his left
eye; another took him full on the nose. He
felt nothing after the first smashing impact,
his face numbed by the force of the blow,
but he was conscious of blood draining over
his mouth, dripping off his chin.

Bradley's mouth gaped, blood trickling
from one corner as his laboring lungs
sucked air, but his onslaught seemed to
intensify. Pat's body shook before the bat-
tering. His left eye was fast closing. Slowly,
he was compelled to back before the slogging assault.

The fists of both men were bloody now,
their shirts red-daubed and their faces
mottled with blood and bruises.

Pat was driven back, back, back until he
could go no further, penned against the bar.
Realization dawned that this toe-to-toe slug-
ging gave all the advantage to his heavier

opponent. Unless he changed his tactics, and changed them fast, the Circle heir would pound him into insensibility. And he knew that Bradley wouldn't quit until he was a helpless mass of bleeding pulp, maybe not even then. This was no ordinary dog-fight, but the accumulation of a lifetime of hate.

Abruptly, he ducked, hurled away from the bar. The intent onlookers surged back to give him space. Bradley swung around, rushed at him like a maddened bull. Pat sidestepped the rush, swung a left against his opponent's ear as Bradley blundered past.

The other staggered, pivoted, bored in again. Pat, more nimble footed, eluded another maddened rush, planting a left into Bradley's paunch.

Jaw sagging as he sucked air, the cowman wheeled, hurtled at him. But Pat had learned his lesson. Darting, dodging, side-stepping, he eluded Bradley's blind rushes, punishing the other with flicking rights and lefts.

Of a sudden, he realized that his opponent was slowing. There was less zip behind the big man's blows; his bleeding mouth gaped wider and wider as he gulped air in sobbing gasps. Conscious of a wild exhilaration, Pat stepped in, aiming for the point of Bradley's jaw.

Too late, he saw a boot swing as, in frantic retaliation, the other launched another frantic kick at his groin.

He swerved, but the swinging boot clipped his right knee. For a moment, the leg was paralyzed. He plunged down and Bradley flung atop him.

Helplessly pinned on his back by the other's weight, Pat was unable to dodge a tornado of short-arm blows that smashed into his face. His mashed nose and torn mouth streamed scarlet. With his one good eye he focused rage. Desperately, he levered his left knee into the other's goin.

He saw Bradley wince. He jerked the knee up, again and again.

Bradley rolled off him, squirmed over the floor, legs doubled up against his belly. Pat levered to his feet and stood swaying, striving to clear his fuzzy brain.

"Boot the bustard!" yelled a man, and a clamor of shouting broke out.

Bradley slowly gathered himself off the floor, swayed toward Pat, swung clumsily. Mustering every ounce of energy he could summon from his battered body, Pat dodged, then stepped close, threw an uppercut at his opponent's jaw. It connected.

50

Bradley shook his head like an angered bull and waded in, arms swinging. But now his movements were slow, clumsy. He swayed on rubbery legs. Pat measured the unsteady form, put everything he had into a left hook under Bradley's jaw. The blow snapped the big man's head up. He staggered backward. Pat dove in, planted a left into his palpitating belly, swung a right at the sagging mouth.

As heavy and limp as a pole-axed steer, Bradley went down, lay sprawled on his back, split lips gaping, face a bloody smear, nose twisted at a grotesque angle. He made no effort to rise, just lay bubbling blood, a helpless, battered hulk.

Pat was in little better shape. He weaved to the nearest chair and collapsed upon it. Someone brought a wet bar rag and he listlessly wiped off his mauled features. Tension suddenly eased; a babble of excited talk broke out among the spectators. Pat saw his opponent's sagging form half dragged, half carried outside, the foreman on one side, a puncher on the other. Deputy Sheriff Bailey had already slipped away. He didn't figure any official action was called for.

Sunlight spearing through the open window of the hotel room aroused Pat the following morning. He sat up, repressing a groan at the protest of bruised ribs. Padding across the worn carpet, he wryly surveyed himself in the mirror set above the washstand. His left eye was buried behind swollen yellow-black flesh; his nose seemed to have flattened and was caked with dried blood; his lips were cut and swollen and felt like chunks of rubber.

"That son-of-a-gun sure worked me over," he murmured ruefully, and spilled water from a pitcher into the wash bowl.

The clerk at the desk said nothing when he dropped down to the lobby, but from the man's quick, interested glance, the rider guessed that the fight was being rehashed all over. There were few secrets in a cow-town and gossip was one of the main ingredients of everyday life.

He swallowed two cups of scalding coffee at the restaurant, but postponed eating — it was just too painful with cut lips and loosened teeth.

Then, for want of something better to do, he wandered down street and dropped into The Wagon Wheel. Another apron, a fat, balding man, was washing glasses behind the bar. At that early hour, the place was bare of patrons.

The barkeep apparently knew about the

fracas. He favored Pat with a wide grin and set a bottle of bourbon on the bar, spun a glass after it. "On the house," he said. "I guess you earned it."

Pat spilled a brief drink, carried it to a table in the rear, near the closed door of Ace's office. Right then he wished to remain as inconspicuous as possible. His mouth and nose would soon return to normal, but that eye! He sighed. He'd likely pack it around for a week or more, like a badge.

The batwings banged back. He glanced up and straightened in his chair with startled recognition. There was no mistaking Bull Bradley's craggy features, the sweep of a rock-like jaw that clamped his mouth tight as a beartrap. Recessed beneath shaggy brows, the old cowman's green eyes reflected a harsh intolerance. The face was that of a tyrant, but there was not a weak spot on it.

In contrast to his son, the cowman wore the working garb of a cowhand — a wrinkled gray shirt and earth-stained Levis thrust into the tops of high boots. A shapeless Stetson was jammed upon his head and a gunbelt sagged around his waist. Dominance and unconscious arrogance sparked his demeanor as he jingled up to the bar.

"Ace around?" he snapped.

The bald barkeep nodded toward the closed door beside which Pat sat.

Bull swung around and headed for the rear of the saloon. As he drew close, his glance lit upon Pat. He jerked to a stop, coldly saw the rider's damaged features. "So you're the fool who hashed up Matt?" he grated.

# VI

Pat sat coolly eying the gnarled Circle boss. "No one names my paw a low-down coyote," he retorted.

"I'm naming him a low-down rustler," barked Bull.

"And I'm tagging you a liar!" returned the rider. His right hand dropped down, brushing the butt of his holstered .45. Tensed, he waited for the cowman to explode into flaming action. But Bull never moved a muscle, just stood weighing the challenger.

Then, with a snort, the cowman moved to the door of Ace's office. Omitting the courtesy of knocking, he flung the door open, stalked inside and slammed the door behind him.

The door banged shut, but the latch failed to engage, and it remained ajar. Pat heard the cowman's rasping demand: "You quit taking Matt's I.O.U.s!" And the saloon man's smooth reply: "Then maybe you'll persuade the colt to quit playing poker."

"The boy's neck-deep in debt," roared Bull, "and I'm through bailing him out."

"Why rawhide me," retorted Ace. "Lay down the law to Matt. Once he yanks a chair up to a card table wild horses couldn't drag him away."

At this point, Pat guessed that the saloon man had indicated that the door was partially open. Abruptly, it closed with a bang.

The closed door shut off sound of the talk within, but Pat could hear Bull's muffled roar, rising and falling, like the mutter of distant thunder, and the murmur of Ace's well-modulated tones.

Of a sudden, the door was wrenched open and the cowman strode out, plainly in a consuming rage. His weathered features were flushed and his thick neck glowed sullen red. Glancing neither to right or left, he forged toward the batwings. Midway across the saloon, Pat detected a break in his stiff-legged stride. He jerked to a stop, clapped a hand to his chest, staggered to a nearby table and sank onto a chair. There he lumped, features contorted, fighting for breath.

Pat jumped up and hurried toward him. The barkeep grabbed a bottle and glass, hastily rounded the end of the bar. When Pat reached the stricken man's side the apron had poured a glass half full of bourbon and was tendering the liquor to Bull. The cowman feebly waved it aside, fumbled in a pocket of his loose-hanging vest, brought out a small tablet. He slipped this into his mouth and sat unmoving, staring at the floor. The tablet seemed to bring relief. He drew a deep breath; signs of pain were removed from his face.

While Pat watched silently and the barkeep stood, partially filled glass in one hand, bottle in the other, the cowman rose, jingled to the batwings and pushed through. Both men stared after him. Ace's voice brought their heads around. The saloon man was standing at the door of his office, puffing a cheroot.

"I'll lay ten to one they plant the old moseyhorn within the month," he said.

"What in thunder hit him?" asked Pat.

"His ticker's acting up. Doc been treating him for heart trouble for months."

Pat wandered outside, paused beneath the wooden saloon awning, gazed up and down street. There were few signs of activity. Dust settled behind Bull Bradley, astride a roan, riding out of town.

The rich aroma of horse manure greeted his nostrils as he strode through the wide doorway of the barn. He slipped a macarty on the claybank, led it from its stall, tied it out in the runway and began working on its coat with currycomb and brush.

Bearded Swede Jorgenson emerged from the tackroom, stumped unhurriedly toward him over the loose planks. The liveryman had one stiff leg. He leaned against a stall, chewing a straw and watching Pat.

"You got nothing better to do than curry a cow pony?" he inquired in his harsh, gutteral voice.

"There's worse ways of killing time," said Pat, and switched the subject. "You wise that Bull Bradley's heart's on the bum?"

"Me and the whole town," returned Swede. "It bucks when the old moseyhorn gets riled up."

"It bucked in The Wagon Wheel not thirty minutes back."

"I guess Bull was raising his hackles over Matt's poker debts," said the liveryman. "They tell me the old man's continual locking horns with the colt over his drinking and gambling debts." He spat. "Matt's rotten, right through! If his paw checks out, he'll tear down in a month what it took Bull twenty years to build. Between rustlers and that good-for-nothing young buzzard, Bull sure got a bellyful of trouble."

Pat's ribs ached like sore teeth as he plied the currycomb. "You asking me to weep?" he inquired acidly.

"Bull ain't all bad," returned Swede defensively. He slapped his stiff leg. "I rode for the Circle when Adobe Wells was a trading post — just one adobe and a barn. Kiowas hit us regular with the full moon. An arrow skewered that knee. It ain't generally known, but Bull set me up in this livery."

Pat eyed the bearded hostler with frowning surprise. "Bull?"

"Yep — Bull," said Swede, and limped away.

Pat led the claybank back to its stall, brought a measure of grain and dumped it in the feed box, then he strolled outside, hunkered in shrinking shadow in front of the barn and made a cigarette.

Swede's talk had set off a new train of thought. Rustlers seemed to be plaguing the Basin, particularly the big Circle spread. Matt was a no-good son of a gun, buried in poker debts. He hated the Harpers. Could be he was heading a gang of rustlers, stealing his own father blind to raise dinero for the tables. And could be he'd grabbed a chance to point the finger at old Jake, to avoid any chance of suspicion that he was involved in the brand-blotching, and, at the same time, avenge past grievances against the Harpers. It seemed a reasonable surmise.

The musing rider was conscious of growing excitement. At last he had something concrete to work on. But Jake was dead; he couldn't help. If Matt had driven that bunch of steers into the canyon nearby the Harper place and worked the brands over, there likely were no witnesses.

There was only one way to get Matt Bradley, he thought. *Join the rustlers.* Then, if his suspicions proved out, he could gather evidence that would send Matt to jail where he belonged.

Pat's bruised features creased into a wry grin. Matt would be no more likely to hire him than he would a rattlesnake. Thoughtfully, he made another cigarette as a plan shaped in his mind.

There wasn't much to the railway depot at Adobe Wells, dangling at the end of a branch line. Shiny spur tracks threaded through a network of cattle pens. A single track snaked northward, skirting the Aridos Hills, to connect with the main line of the Kansas & Rio Grande at Bonita, seat of Bonita County.

When Pat entered the depot and peered through the ticket window, the depot agent slacked at a table untidy with a litter of papers. Stoically, a man accustomed to loneliness, he was sucking a pipe and listlessly leafing through a dogeared magazine. At the jingle of Pat's spur chains, his head came around.

"Telegram!" said Pat, thrusting a sheet of paper through the opening.

Thrusting a green eyeshade up into graying hair, the agent extended a hand. He read aloud, checking the words with a pencil:

*Hoot Fuller, General Delivery, Amarillo, Texas. Meet me Adobe Wells Hotel, Big Basin pronto.*
*Pat.*

"Nine words," said the agent. "That'll be two dollars."

Pat pushed three silver dollars through the window. "Buy yourself a drink," he said, "and button up."

"Sure will!" said the man, his eyes brightening. "Ain't you Jake Harper's boy?"

"Yep!"

"Too bad about that hanging," mused the agent. "Plenty cowmen in the Basin got their start with a running iron." He eyed

61

Pat's damaged optic and bruised features with a grin. "Wal, I see you did something about it."

It was plain the agent connected the saloon fight with the hanging, like everyone else in town, thought Pat. Guess they were all waiting for his next move. He'd gamble they'd never guess what he had in mind.

Three days later, after sundown, he was stretched on his bed, absorbing the contents of *The Bonita County Bulletin* by the mellow light of an oil lamp set on the scratched bureau. His gunbelt decorated a bedpost, his hat hooked on another, his boots sat by the bed.

The door was knuckled sharply. "Come in!" he bawled.

The handle turned and a sober-faced rider about his own age, clanked over the threshold. He was taller than Pat, stringy, with deadpan features, wistful brown eyes and an owlish squint that gave the impression that he was in a perpetual state of bewilderment. Which impression was decidly erroneous, for Hoot Fuller was a shrewd young man and an adroit horse trader.

Years back, the two had gravitated together when they met as cowhands on a Neuces River spread. From the first they'd hit it off and teamed up. Deciding that nursing cows offered no future, they'd launched several ventures, all of which left them flat. However, both were of a type that was spurred by setbacks and they'd finally hit the jackpot in the shape of a horse ranch. Hoot, Pat knew from experience, was a pard he could bank on through hell and high water.

His visitor paused, eying Pat's blackened eye and damaged features with interest. "Seems someone beat me to it," he commented. "I was all set to administer the same. What in thunder got into you — busting out of the corral, then dragging me across all creation?"

He dropped onto the only chair and fished out the makin's. "You in a tight or something?"

"Nope," said Pat. "But I could use a good rustler!"

Hoot groaned. "You loco, playing games? We got an Army contract — remember?"

"You're the biggest crook I know," said Pat, "and I reckon we got two good hands in Jose and Pedro. They'll go ahead breaking them broomtails." He threw the newspaper aside, sat up and reached for Hoot's makin's. "Now listen!"

He told of the events that had brought

him back to Big Basin: the feud between the Harpers and Bradleys, his suspicion that old Jake had been framed by Matt Bradley. "I got a hanging to avenge," he concluded tightly. "All I crave is to put Matt Bradley where he belongs, and the only way to tag the lobo is to join that rustling gang."

"If you can't whip 'em — join 'em," supplied Hoot.

"I can't join 'em," retorted Pat. "Matt got no more use for me than a hydrophobia skunk. You now — you're a stranger."

"So I qualify to dangle on a rope," murmured the other. He shook his head. "I got a yen to stick to horse breaking — it's healthier."

"Quit acting ornery," begged Pat, "and listen. This is how I've got it figured."

# VII

It was pay day on the ranches and The Wagon Wheel was a droning hive of conviviality. Saddle stiffs from the Circle, Window Sash, Cross C, Pothook and other spreads crowded the tables and lined the bar. Among the latter was Matt Bradley, conscious of amused glances directed at his healing scars and still misshapen nose. He was in no good humor.

To his side eased a stringy rider with an owl-like squint. "Reckon you could use a good hand on the Circle, Mister Bradley?" he inquired earnestly.

"Just how good you figure you are?" growled Matt, eying him with no friendliness.

"Good enough to team up with Pat Harper, running wet stock across the Rio," replied Hoot. He added hastily, "My rope ain't sticky no more."

"So Pat contracted his Old Man's bad

habits!" barked the Circle heir. He scowled at the anxious-eyed cowpoke. "Chew on this, feller — the Circle ain't hiring no reformed rustlers, and, what's more, any hombre who'd team up with a Harper stinks. Beat it, afore I sic the law onto you."

Hoot hastily faded into the press of yammering punchers thronging the floor. Shortly after, he slipped out of the saloon and headed for the hotel. Here he dolefully reported his failure to Pat, in the latter's room.

"Guess the whole idea was crazy," frowned Pat. "If I had the brains of a canary bird, I'd have known that Matt's not taking any chances cutting a drifting saddlebum into a slick rustling gang. Sorry I tolled you down from Amarillo, Hoot."

"Quit acting as sad as a feever-ticked dogie," advised his pard, dropping onto the chair and stretching his long legs. "You figure this Matt hombre would tip his hand to a stranger? Give the bustard time to chew on it. I'll stick around town awhile, Maybe he'll bite yet."

"And if he don't bite?"

"We'll figure another angle," returned Hoot confidently. "Now perk up and dig out that deck of marked cards you use to beggar me."

Pat brought out the pasteboards and a bottle. They played two-handed euchre on the bed until close upon midnight. Then, the bottle empty, they called it a day.

Pat had scarcely shucked his boots and pants, blown out the lamp and stretched out to sleep when he heard the door rattle slightly, as though someone out in the corridor was trying to ease into the room. Since he had jammed the back of the straightback chair beneath the knob, the door remained immovable.

He jerked to a sitting position, staring into the gloom.

There was a quiet, guarded knock on the door. He reached for his .45, thumbed back the hammer, swung off the bed and padded to the door.

Again it was knuckled, more insistently.

He jerked the chair away, threw open the door and, gun leveled waist high, stared at Jules Garrott, rawboned segundo of the Circle B.

A lamp, turned low, was in the corridor. By its faint light, Pat stood eying the swarthy features of the foreman with wide-eyed amazement. Garrot touched a hand to his lips to indicate silence and stepped past him into the room.

Perplexed, Pat closed the door, struck a

stinker and touched it to the wick of the lamp. As yellow flame blossomed, Garrott crossed the room and yanked down the window shade.

Gun still latched in his fist, Pat watched, forehead creased.

"Ditch that hoglaig!" grunted Garrott.

"Not when you pack a .45," threw back Pat, his mind in a whirl as he speculated as to the reason for this midnight visit.

The foreman shrugged, dropped onto the chair and fished out the makin's.

Pat perched gingerly on the edge of the disordered bed, gun slack in his right hand. "What in thunder brought you here?" he asked.

"Business!"

"What kind of business?"

"Rustling."

"Maybe you should cut the deck a mite deeper," suggested Pat, his eyes searching the foreman's high-boned, swarthy features.

Garrott touched a match to a brown paper cigarette. "It seems," he returned carefully, "that you and a gent who braced Matt in the saloon been running wet stock across the Rio Grande."

"So?"

Garrott raised his shoulders. "There's a slug of dinero to be picked up running stock right here."

It was all clear enough to Pat now — Matt Bradley rodded the rustlers. Garrott was his right-hand man. Anxious to remain in the background, Matt had steered Garrott to the hotel for the purpose of adding a couple of new men to the gang. Excitement stirred him. At the most, he'd hoped that Hoot might be admitted to the gang, but it seemed that this was his lucky day. Matt must sure be hard up for men to sink his animosity.

Cautiously, he said, "The Harpers got a bad reputation in the Basin."

"Don't let that faze you," returned Garrott carelessly. "You won't be around. We got the Basin pretty well organized. What we need is hombres to haze the stuff across the border."

"We!" repeated Pat. "Who's holding cards in this deal?"

"What's it to you?" challenged the foreman. "You get yours."

"Just what do I get?"

"A dollar a head, for a two day drive." Faint belligerence edged Garrott's tone. "I gamble you didn't pick up that kind of easy money on the River."

"It ain't chickenfeed," agreed Pat. He reached and dropped his sixgun into the

69

holster of the belt dangling from the bed post. Then he rose and began pacing the threadbare square of carpet. If he grabbed at the offer, he reflected, the foreman's suspicions might be aroused. Lady Luck had dealt aces, but he had to play them right. Puffing his smoke, Garrott slacked on the chair, sharp eyes following every movement of the pacing rider.

Pat turned suddenly. "You pay off on delivery?"

"We sure do," rasped the other. "In six months you'll pocket enough dinero to burn a wet mule."

"Hunky-dory!" exclaimed Pat abruptly. "Count me in!"

"Your pard, too?"

"Sure," said Pat carelessly, "Hoot'll go along."

Garrott ground his butt into the carpet and rose. "Now," he grated, "this is what you do.

When the jingle of the foreman's spur chains died down the corridor, Pat doused the lamp, moved quickly to the window and jerked up the shade. Outside, the moon was near full and laid a sheen of silver on square-fronted stores.

By the hitchrail outside, a yellow-haired

rider, hat thrust back, sat the saddle, a riderless pony on the lead. His features were red
and square, and smoke drifted from a
cigarette between his lips. Then Jules Garrott stepped into the saddle of the led pony.
For several minutes, the two traded low-
voiced talk. Then they parted, riding in different directions.

The new day was no more than a red stain
on the eastern horizon and Adobe Wells still
slept in a pool of shadow when Pat and
Hoot headed out of town. They deemed it
good business to slip away as quietly as possible. Bones Bailey, the deputy, had a sharp
eye and an uncanny habit of divining mo-
tives.

Growing light slowly erased the stars as
their ponies jogged across the flats toward
the vague bulk of the Aridos Hills. The
hideout where Garrott had told Pat to
report lay deep in the hills, a dozen miles
beyond the old Harper place.

As they rode stirrup to stirrup through
the coolness of dawn, the plain around them
rolling away into obscurity, Pat told his pard
of the city folks who had taken over his
father's holding.

"The gent ain't such-a-much, but the
girl!" He paused to compose a fitting de-

scription of May Matthews. "A queen! Soft and pretty as a young calf's ears."

Hoot yawned. "Fluffy and helpless," he said. "Speaking personal, city gals ain't my dish. I've seen 'em in mail order catalogs showing off their forms in corsets. Reckon they ain't good for much more."

"You've got May all wrong," Pat assured him earnestly. "She's sweet as a bee tree. She cooks, keeps house. And her shape!" He made expressive curves with both hands.

"You forgot the wings," grunted his pard, "likewise the halo."

"We've got time aplenty to reach that hideaway afore sundown," said Pat. "We'll drop in and say howdy. I'm kinda hankering to give her a once-over again. What's more, I've got a five spot that says you'll change your ideas."

"I never was such-a-much for gals," admitted Hoot. "There was a towheaded school ma'am once, near San Antone, but she up and married a Mex trader."

"A Mex! What did he have that you lacked?"

"Dinero!" said Hoot.

It was still early in the day when they rode into the Harper place, but the tubercular Matthews was already seated on the gallery, slapping cards. He glanced up briefly when

72

they pulled rein in front of the house, but favored them with no more than an absent-minded nod.

"Social gent!" commented Hoot in tones that couldn't have failed to reach the invalid's ears. Before Pat could reply, May stepped out of the house, apron tied over her trim house dress, arms dusted white with flour.

"Hello!" she cried gaily. "If my cake's ruined, it will be on your conscience." She stepped out from beneath the canopy, fondled the claybank's head. Her frank gray eyes focused the rider. "This is a pleasant surprise," she confessed. "I thought you'd left the Basin — and forgotten me."

"Forget you!" Pat's ardent gaze dwelt on her slim form. "I just don't think that's possible." He swung out of the saddle.

"Once seen, never forgotten," said Hoot solemnly. The girl darted a quick, puzzled glance at his sober features.

"Meet Hoot Fuller, my pard," said Pat. "And don't let his wisecracks faze you. Guess Hoot was just born that way, like a five-legged hog."

May laughed and turned to the owlish rider. "It's real nice to meet you, Hoot. You sure don't look like a five-legged hog to me."

"They raise all the hogs in Big Basin," said

Hoot. "But they sure planted a pretty rose right here." He grinned. "Right now, I've got the feeling like I'm fifth wheel on a wagon."

He reached for the headstall of Pat's pony. "Reckon I'll water these broncs and slack cinches while you two trade talk." He drifted away with the led horse.

May eyed Pat, a twinkle in her eyes. "You forgot to tell me your friend is tactful, too."

"Let's take a pacer!" he urged. She glanced uncertainly in the direction of the man hunched on the porch laying out cards, then nodded.

Side by side, they strolled toward the pasture, saying nothing. Finally, the girl broke a silence that was becoming strained. "So you're staying in the Basin?"

"For awhile," he admitted, adding quickly, "I'm turning rustler."

"You're — what?" she jerked to a stop and swung around, facing him, eyes wide with surprise.

He grinned. "Sounds crazy, don't it?"

"It is crazy!" she declared emphatically. "Have you forgotten what happened to your father?"

"Paw was no rustler!"

She raised her shoulders with a gesture of exasperated resignation.

"I know the Old Man was clean," he assured her fervently. "You folks are strangers around here. You don't know the Basin. The Harpers and Bradleys been feuding for a generation. Matt Bradley framed Paw."

"Matt Bradley!"

"Yep, Matt," he assured her grimly. "I figure that Matt rods a rustling gang. He's looting the Circle and other ranches blind. When he hanged Paw he downed two bucks with one shot — he got rid of a Harper and he covered up his own operations."

Throughout, the girl stood absorbed, lips parted, eyes incredulous. "But why would Matt steal cows," she objected. "He's heir to a big ranch; the Bradleys are wealthy. He doesn't lack money."

Pat laughed shortly. "Matt's bogged down in poker debts. What's more, Bull quit paying his I.O.U.s."

They moved on again, skirting the barbed wire fence of the pasture. Glancing back, Pat saw that Hoot was hunkered by the water trough, smoking. The head of the invalid on the gallery was raised, he was following their progress.

"Why would Matt hire you — his enemy?" the girl asked suddenly.

"He didn't," chuckled Pat. "Jules Garrott, his right bower, propositioned me. Couldbe

Matt hasn't wised up yet."

"So your object in joining these rustlers," she commented thoughtfully, "is to expose their operations."

"Sure!"

"And so be revenged upon Matt Bradley."

"You hit the bull's-eye."

"I think you would be better advised to leave the Basin and let sleeping dogs lie," she said quietly.

"That's because you are a girl — a sweet, soft-hearted girl," he returned, and impulsively slipped an arm around her slim waist, drew her close and pressed a kiss squarely upon her red lips. She wrenched away, features flushed, and her head swiveled quickly toward the form bent over the card table on the gallery.

"You shouldn't have done that," she protested breathlessly.

"What's wrong with a kiss?"

"Judd — my father — has strict ideas."

"What does he figure you are — a nun?"

"It's not that," she was recovering her aplomb now. "It's just that his illness makes him — difficult." She turned away and began briskly walking back toward the house. He hastened after her, caught up and paced beside her. "Say, May," he said, "I'm real sorry."

"Suppose we forget the whole thing," she returned shortly, eyes straight ahead.

When they approached the house, Hoot came to his feet and became busy tightening cinches. The invalid was engrossed with his card game. Pat, with an irritated glance at the girl, headed for his pony. She crossed the gallery and entered the adobe without a backward glance.

"You forget to kiss her goodbye?" said Hoot, features bland.

Pat snorted and swung into leather.

When the two breasted the rim of the bowl, Pat glanced back, as he had on his previous visit, but there was no fluttering handkerchief this time, no sign of the girl, nothing except the stooped form of Judd Matthews flicking cards. Tight-lipped, he roweled the claybank, shot ahead.

"What in creation got into you?" demanded Hoot.

"Guess I tangled my spurs — with May," confessed Pat glumly.

"Uncertain, coy, and hard to please," murmured Hoot. "I read that in a book."

"They're sure hard to figure," admitted Pat.

"That goes for her old man," chuckled his pard. "When you two were smooching, I'd swear he was gritting his teeth like he could eat the sights off a sixgun. At that," he added thoughtfully, "it would be a pleasure to lamp that gal modeling one of them mail order corsets."

# VIII

The two riders pushed deeper into a chaos of upended terrain, a barren malpais of wind-scoured rock, twisted canyons and heaped talus. This arid wilderness was the last place a cowman would comb for rustled stock, thought Pat, and he'd need a mighty fine-toothed comb to do any kind of a job. Cows needed water as well as grass, which was why so few strays wandered into the Aridos Hills. His own father had emptied one of the few known springs. But there was other water, he had little doubt about that. In past days, bands of Indians had lurked in this rugged wilderness with their women and children and animals. Secret springs gave them life. It was a sure bet that the rustlers had located one of those springs.

They hit the hideaway unexpectedly. Hoot drew rein with a low whistle. "Ain't that a sight for sore eyes!" he exclaimed.

Before them stretched a narrow valley,

hemmed in by steep, boulder-freckled slopes. Chaparral-veined on one side, its verdant green was soothing after the sun-seared tumult of rock through which they had been threading. The floor of the valley, carpeted with sparse grass, was destitute of trees, save for a solitary scrub oak. Across it, perhaps two hundred head of stock were scattered, grazing peacefully.

"I can scarce believe it," mused Hoot. "Who'd figure on running plumb into grazing stock in this devil's dumping ground?"

"No one," said Pat. "That's howcome they're here."

The two lifted their reins and began to drift down into the valley. A sharp challenge hit their ears. Both halted abruptly, heads turning in the direction of the voice.

A steeple-topped hat protruded above a clutter of rock, and beneath it the swarthy features of a vaquero. The sun glinted on the steel barrel of a rifle propped on a shoulder of a boulder, and lined on them.

"Jules Garrott sent us!" yelled Pat.

The lookout came to his feet, Winchester still leveled in his hands. He was a sturdy fellow, a tangle of dark hair curling from beneath his sombrero. His pocked features creased into a grin.

*"Buenos dias, senors!"* he returned. "We

had word of your coming."

Carelessly cradling the Winchester beneath an arm, he sauntered toward them. "They call me Sancho," he volunteered.

"My handle's Harper," threw back Pat. "This gent's Hoot."

The vaquero began fashioning a cornhusk cigarette while his dark eyes dwelt on Hoot's solemn features. "Wise, like an owl?" he inquired, with a flash of white teeth.

"You can't tell a hoss by its coat," said Pat.

Sancho seemed a friendly cuss. Like many of his kind, his taste went to geegaws. Tiny silver conchas tinkled around the broad brim of his sombrero; huge silvered rowels hitched behind his riding boots and his gunbelt was thickly inlaid with silver studs. He wore a dirty yellow silk shirt and dusty dark pants. In addition to the Winchester, he packed a sixgun and a sheathed knife. His features were broad, good-humored, but his dark eyes held a lurking furtiveness. Such men as these, thought Pat, riding beyond the law, could never wholly banish the specter of a hangrope.

"Guess we'll mosey along," he said, and raised his reins.

The lookout waved careless farewell. *"Vaya con Dios!"* he called, and wandered back to the nest of rock.

As the two jogged across the valley floor, Pat eyed the brands of the feeding steers. "These gents sure spread a wide loop," he commented. "Circle, Sash, Pothook, Cross. They sure ain't choosy. All prime stuff, too."

Approaching the chaparral, they glimpsed a pole corral and a rude cabin, rock-walled, chinked with mud. Beyond, the cliff face angled up, too steep for ascent. Its base was dappled green with moss and spiderwebbed with an infinity of cracks. Below, the water pooled among a tumble of boulders, the run-off meandering along the foot of the cliff, smothered with lush growth.

Blue jays called raucously from crumbling ledges; humming birds darted through the sunlight; whiptail lizards skittered among the fallen talus.

A saddle horse stood droop-hipped by the corral. Close by, a gray-shirred rider tended a pot suspended over glowing coals in a rock fireplace. Two blanket rolls lumped on the ground.

Although the rider by the fire must have heard sound of their approach, he paid no attention as they rode up to the corral, dismounted and slacked cinches.

Pat approached the fire. "You Dakota?" he drawled.

The rider straightened and turned. Thin lips compressed, he weighed Pat with frosty eyes. He was wire-thin, with a long, stubbled jaw and beady-black eyes that glittered between narrowed slits. There was not a touch of color about him, from dirt-grimed jeans to battered Stetson. He wore his gun in a flared holster, thonged down. *A gray old lobo,* thought Pat, *watchful, tensed, suspicious — always suspicious.*

"So you're the two roosters Jules saddled me with!" The rustler's tone held sour contempt. His glance flicked to the gun bumping Pat's right leg. "What you pack that hawgleg for — ornament?"

"You crave to find out?" inquired Pat shortly.

The thin-faced Dakota considered this silently, then he jerked his head in the direction of a sooted coffeepot set in the coals. "Pour yourself a mug of dip," he growled, and moved away.

Several tin mugs lay around. Pat picked up one and blew out the dust. Hoot grabbed another. Pat spilled steaming black liquid from the coffeepot into each. "Lamp the mirror!" he told his pard, nodding at a small fragment of looking glass on the fireplace. "That hairpin watched every move we made, from the start."

"You ain't saying he don't trust us?" inquired Hoot plaintively.

"I'd say he scarce trusts himself."

Nursing their steaming mugs, the two moved over to the shade of a stunted cedar and hunkered. Dakota had stepped into the cabin.

"Nice, friendly cuss," commented Pat.

"What did you expect — a kiss?" queried Hoot, and shook his head sadly. "I guess you still got that sweet little hunk of sugar candy on your mind."

"All I got on my mind right now," grunted Pat, "is them steers. How you figure they drove 'em in without leaving sign?"

"In small chunks," returned Hoot promptly. "Maybe switching trails continuous. Who'd hunt for sign back in here, anyway?"

They found there was little to do in the hideaway beyond spelling Sancho as lookout. As Hoot had guessed, stock was continually dribbled in by strange riders, never more than half a dozen steers to a bunch.

Dakota proved to be — as Hoot expressed it — as techy as a tomcat. The rustler spoke little, craved nothing but his own company, but his beady eyes, always questing restlessly, missed nothing.

Sancho, his helper, on the other hand, was friendly as a puppy. Plainly glad of other company than that of the taciturn Dakota, he hung around the newcomers, always eager to trade talk, oblivious of Dakota's scowling disapproval.

By dint of casual questioning, they learned that he never left the valley, but remained in the hideaway to handle the steady inflow of steers. He confided to Hoot that this suited him well — he was dodging a warrant for knifing a deputy sheriff in a saloon fracas, and a rope likely awaited him outside.

Furthermore, he confided that the gang had members planted in most of the Basin spreads, riding as punchers. Their job was to steer the rustlers onto likely bunches of stock and acquaint them with movements of night guards.

When stock gathered in the hideaway tallied four hundred or so, the rustled steers were trailed south, across the border. Dakota was trail boss and two rustlers from the Basin usually rode with him.

South of the border, the boss had buyers ready and waiting to hand over ten dollars gold for every prime steer. Jules visited the hideaway when Dakota returned from each drive, took charge of the gold, and paid off.

"So Jules is the big man!" commented Pat.

Sancho shook his head in vigorous negation. "I theenk no. Once when Dakota have question, Jules say wait 'til he ask boss. Jules is segundo. The boss?" He spread his hands and shrugged.

So his guess had been right, considered Pat. Matt rodded the outfit. Had to give the Circle heir credit. He sure had built up a jim-dandy organization. It was hard to believe Bull's dissipated son had the brains and go-gettem. Seems he had more of his father's qualities than appeared on the surface.

Night closed in on the hideaway on the evening of the second day. Hoot was on lookout. The remaining three hunkered around the fire, Sancho, as usual, chattering. Pat listened and Dakota gloomily chewed a cigarette and stared at the dancing flames. Suddenly, Dakota said, "We move out at sunup."

Sancho checked in the midst of his voluable discourse and stared at the bitter-faced rustler, jaw slack with surprise.

*"Que diablo!"* he exclaimed. "You cannot make the drive; we have but half of a herd."

"Boss sent word," returned Dakota shortly. "Me and the two mavericks'll handle what we got." He glowered at Pat. "And keep that trigger finger greased!

Border scum highjacked one herd."

Pat rubbed his chin, considering. Dakota would have a real shock, he reflected, if the sour-faced rustler knew that this herd was due to be highjacked — by the law. But how was he to get word to the law before sunup?"

In the gloom beyond the flickering circle of firelight a bit chain jingled. Hoot rode in, swung out of leather by the corral. Sancho straightened and headed for his pony, jogged into the night to take post as guard.

Hoot sauntered over, dropped down by the fire, began to build a smoke.

"We're moving out," said Pat, "at sunup."

"Ain't that nice!" Hoot reached for a blazing twig, touched it to his cigarette. "Maybe I'll find me a nice dark-eyed senorita below the border."

"I got a senorita right in the Basin I crave to spark afore we hit the trail," returned Pat.

"Wal, who's setting on your shirt?" threw back Hoot.

"No one leaves camp!" rasped Dakota from across the fire.

"I've got different ideas," announced Pat coolly, and came to his feet.

Dakota straightened, too. The firelight washed over his thin, frowning features. "You stay right here!" he decreed, and his right hand dropped to the butt of his holstered gun.

Hoot had slipped out his Colt. Hunkered, he nursed it in his lap. In the taut silence that followed Dakota's declaration, sound of a metallic clink as loud as a hammer was thumbed back.

Dakota's wary gaze flicked downward. The eight inch barrel of Hoot's sixgun slanted in his direction, aligned on his chest. "Ain't it funny," mused the owlish rider, "how these thumb-busters are liable to spout lead, accidently like." He looked up, gazing blandly at the fuming Dakota. "Wouldn't it be too bad now, if my thumb slipped?"

"So you two roosters are ganging up on me!" choked the rustler.

"Heck, Pat craves to cuddle his gal," returned Hoot plaintively.

Dakota glowered at Pat. "You sashay down into the Basin and Jules'll nail your hide to the barn," he promised starkly.

"Let's leave that to Jules," returned Pat offhand. He turned and moved off into the darkness. Dakota, shaking with frustrated anger, stood staring after him. Again he glanced at the pointed gun in Hoot's fist, itching with indecision.

"Set down!" directed the rider, and his tone had lost its easy banter. "Pat's crazy over that gal."

With slow reluctance, Dakota again hunkered. "Mister," he promised thinly, "I'll have your scalp for this, both your scalps!"

"I was born bald-headed," murmured Hoot. "Why in thunder couldn't I have kept that way?" He squinted across the fire at the bitter-faced rustler's scowling features. "When we hit the border, let's you and me hunt up a couple of chiquitas."

"The hell with you and your chiquitas!" barked Dakota. "Quit fussing with that dog-goned gun."

# IX

It was nearing midnight when Pat rode into Adobe Wells. Main Street was a canyon of darkness through which lighted windows of rooms on the second floor of the hotel pricked like peering eyes. The only other sign of life was supplied by ponies standing hipshot outside The Wagon Wheel.

Outside the deputy's office, Pat pulled to the rail, glancing up and down the shadowed plankwalk. No one seemed to be around. He tied the claybank and knuckled the door.

At his rap, he heard a rustle inside. The door eased open a scant six inches. "Wal?" inquired the deputy's nasal voice.

"I crave to talk — confidential," said Pat quickly. "No light!"

The door swung open and he stepped into darkness. He heard the door close behind him, sound of Bones padding around. A match scratched. Light blossomed.

"Douse it!" he snapped, but the deputy

calmly touched fire to a stable lamp, reached up and hooked it by the bail to a viga overhead.

"I ain't no owl," grunted the deputy, "and quit fretting; the windows are covered."

Pat's quick glance sought the two small windows. Each was draped with a square of blanket.

"You ain't the first hombre took a notion to drop in after dark," said Bones. He dropped onto a chair, brought out his corncob pipe and stuffed the bowl. "Wal, what's itching you?" he asked.

Tersely, Pat told of his talk with the doctor. In his weakened state, he pointed out, it would have been close to impossible for Jake to have rustled the steers for which he was hanged. Further, the five hundred dollars gold came from the sale on his holding to the Matthews.

Silently listening, the gangling deputy sat chewing his pipestem, flintly eyes veiled.

"I figure," said Pat, at the end of the recital, "Matt Bradley framed Paw — he never had any use for a Harper. What's more, Matt's back of the Basin rustling."

"You been chewing loco weed?" inquired Bones with obvious disbelief. It was plain he considered the accusation was triggered by Pat's feud with the Circle heir.

"I've got proof!" insisted the rider, and explained how Hoot Fuller had braced Matt, the midnight visit of Garrott that followed, his joining the gang to gather evidence that would expose Matt Bradley. Now he could see that the old deputy's attention was quickening.

"It's plain as the ears on a mule," asserted Pat. "Garrott hired me, and Garrott's Matt's right bower. We're pushing a bunch of rustled stock south at sunup." His voice rose with excitement. "There'll be a stopover at Coyote Spring. You get there first with a posse and you'll recover a slew of steers, and likewise corral a gent named Dakota. Then we pick up Sancho in the hideaway and I gamble either one of the other will spill his guts. We've got the goods on Garrott; we'll nail down Matt, too."

Bones tapped his pipe. He seemed amused. "I already swore in a posse," he said. "By noon tomorrow they'll be waiting at Coyote Spring."

Pat stared. "Who — how —" he began.

Wordlessly, the deputy reached for his vest, hanging from a peg, lifted a folded paper from a pocket. The dry sheet crackled as he opened it and handed it to his visitor.

With growing bewilderment, Pat read:

PAT HARPER, WITH OTHER RUSTLERS, IS RUNNING A HERD OF STOLEN STOCK SOUTH ON FRIDAY. THEY WATER AT COYOTE SPRING.

The note was written in pencil, the words printed in block capitals. There was no signature.

Pat gulped and looked up. "How in thunder did you get hold of this?" he demanded.

"Slid under the door," said Bones, "sometime last night, I reckon."

"Who in hell would send it?"

"Someone who craves your scalp, I guess," the deputy told him dryly.

"But no one, outside of Matt and Garrott, is wise we're pushing the stuff south," protested Pat. Then understanding came. "So that's it!" he commented, with a tight smile. "Matt's boys usually gather four hundred head or more afore they haze 'em across the border. This trip they got a scant two hundred. When Jules told Matt he'd hired me, that dirty double-crossing son figured he'd throw away a few cows just so he could send me to the pen. That's why we're only trailing half a herd."

"Howcome you're so deadset Matt's behind all these shenanigans?" inquired the deputy.

"Heck!" came back Pat derisively. "Ain't it plain? Matt's neck deep in debt. He hates my guts. He got a yen to corral a sack of dinero."

"If this gang's organized like you say," returned the deputy, "the hombre ramrodding it got plenty savvy. I'd say Matt was as shy of brains as a chicken is of feathers. Jules now! That breed's slick as calves' slobbers. They claim Jules is as good as boss out at the Circle. Bull's out of action, flat on his back. That ticker's real bad. Matt's as useless as a twenty-two cartridge in an eight-gauge shotgun. So Jules rules the roost. What's more, he likes that gal Diane. Bull were to check out, I'd lay a ten spot to a beer the breed marries the gal and takes over complete."

*Jules Garrott marry Diane!* For no good reason, the thought was distasteful to Pat. He just couldn't picture the high-spirited Bradley girl tied up to the swarthy high-cheeked breed.

"So you figure Jules is kingpin!" he commented. "You're barking up the wrong tree, Bones."

"Mebbeso," agreed the deputy placidly. "Wal, see you at Coyote Spring!"

"Couldbe!" grinned Pat. "And couldbe I'll duck out. Watch for Dakota. That gent's a real tarantula."

Galaxies of stars glittering overhead, Pat rode eastward across the swales, cogitating on the mysterious message the deputy had received. It was plain enough to him. Matt had grabbed the opportunity to tole him and Hoot into a trap. Matt would sacrifice the steers and Dakota just for the satisfaction of placing an old enemy behind bars. Likely the beating he took in The Wagon Wheel had added fire to his smoldering hatred. And he — Pat — had laid himself wide open by tying up with the rustlers. If he hadn't grabbed the chance to ride in and tip Bones off, he thought ruefully, likely he would have been buzzard bait before another sundown. Folks would have had no doubt about his guilt. Like father like son! Lady Luck had sure been in a benevolent mood.

Vague light was filtering across fading stars, heralding the approach of dawn when he rode into the hideaway.

Hoot was yawning on lookout. Quickly, Pat told his pard of the talk with the deputy, and of the trap they had come so close to riding into.

"Why didn't I stick to breaking ponies?" groaned Hoot. "Don't rustling call for a ten-year stretch, plaiting hair bridles?"

"In the Basin they stretch your neck," returned Pat. "Wal, I'll drift down to camp and grab what little shuteye's coming."

Dakota and Sancho bulked in their soogans when he stripped the gear off his pony. He yanked off his boots, unbuckled his gunbelt and quickly slid beneath the canvas of his own tarp.

While the narrow valley was still a pool of gray obscurity, the herd threaded through the split in the wall that gave entrance to the hideaway. Winding through canyons and across dry washes, it plodded southward.

When noon approached the herd was still in rough terrain, but the spiny hills were smoothing out and the canyons began to shallow. As the blowing column of cows moved across a high bench, Pat caught a glimpse of the desert washing up to the southern flanks of the Aridos Hills. He pulled off, out of hovering dust, and eyed the purpled expanse. Clumped beargrass and prickly pear crusted the waste. Afar off, dust devils whirled, caught up by vagrant air currents.

The coiling length of the herd began to snake downward toward sagebrush flats that edged the desert. Pat dropped back, watching the lumbering procession of blowing, red-eyed beasts flow by. At the tail of the herd, veiled by a gray fog, Hoot was urging on stragglers with a swinging rope.

At Pat's gesture he pulled out, and the pair sat their ponies, watching the herd wind out of sight, until slow-settling dust that marked their passage blotted the last steers from view.

"This is where we pull out," said Pat. "There'll be a reception committee at Coyote Spring, and it ain't too far ahead."

Hoot smeared sweat and dust from his face. "It ain't too soon for me!"

"Maybe we should find a high spot and kinda keep cases on that herd," decided Pat.

Hoot chuckled at a thought. "I gamble Dakota will be mad enough to chew the sights off his sixgun when he finds we hightailed."

"And there ain't a damned thing he can do about it," put in Pat. "The lobo can't leave the steers."

Westward, the terrain bulged, rising, bench upon bench, to a rugged escarpment. The two set their ponies to the slope, working up the benches. Finally, Pat halted his blowing claybank and turned in the saddle. Almost to his feet, it seemed, lapped the desert. Through the clear air, Coyote Butte seemed almost within rifleshot, although he knew it to be miles distant.

The herd was still hidden somewhere among the tangle of swelling hills below, and he wondered how in creation Dakota would hold it together.

Dismounting, the two slackened cinches and rocked their saddles, then hunkered by the gnarled trunk of a twisted old juniper and settled themselves to wait. Pat was dozing when Hoot's elbow rammed into his ribs. When his head jerked up, the other motioned toward the vast spread of desert below. Crawling across it, like a many-legged centipede, was the herd. Dwarfed by distance, the steers seemed little bigger than ants. Dakota, like a hovering gnat, darted up and down the column. And he had his hands full, reflected Pat. The steers were tiring and the herd fast falling apart. A scattering of animals already lagged far behind, some had turned and were drifting back to the hills.

"Dakota got more troubles than a one armed man with the itch," commented Hoot.

"He's bunching 'em," said Pat, squinting from beneath the brim of his Stetson. "There ain't no other way."

They watched the speck that was Dakota

halt the leaders and head for the drag. Whirling, circling, back-tracking, he began hazing the column into one solid mass.

"I gamble his language is scorching their hides," said Hoot with huge enjoyment.

"You gotta hand it to him," returned Pat. "The hombre's sure no quitter."

Ignoring the stragglers, the lone rider below eventually gathered the cavalcade into a tight herd. It began to drift forward, Dakota racing around its flanks. Its pace quickened.

"They scent water," said Hoot. "Guess his troubles are most over."

"They've scarce begun," amended Pat. "You forgot the posse?"

Gradually, the shape of the moving mass of beef changed into that of a broad arrowhead, slimming as the indefatigable Dakota pushed in the flanks. Then the arrowhead slowly crumbled, losing all semblance of shape, as the more active animals forged ahead, while the lame and the wary dropped behind. But every steer was moving steadily in the same direction — Coyote Butte.

In their rear rode Dakota, swerving as he hazed on the laggards.

The leaders were nearing the Butte now. Pat blinked; he could have sworn he glimpsed a gun flash from the heaped talus that cumbered the base of the pile. The report punched thinly through the air. He saw the darting speck that was Dakota check, remain still, while the scattered herd flowed on.

Abruptly, Dakota wheeled and streaked away from the Butte, leaving the herd.

Tiny forms became visible, riding out from the shadow of the eroding pile, threading through specked steers. Both the men on the high bench were on their feet now, watching intently.

"Some damned fool of a posseman got buck fever and tipped his hand," declared Pat, with disgust.

Absorbed, they watched the scene below — the fleeing Dakota and, far behind him, the toylike forms of his pursuers, strung out in chase. Finally, the fugitive was hidden by intervening ridges.

# X

"It's long odds they'll never corral that lobo, once he reaches the hills," said Hoot.

"And the evidence we needed to pin back Matt Bradley's ears goes up in smoke," returned Pat bitterly, "all because some fool posseman jumped the gun."

"What's more," commented Hoot wryly, "the hairpin will be on our trail."

In a short space of time the dreary stretch of desert below was void of life, except for steers specked around Coyote Butte as possemen pounding on the fleeing rustler's trail were hidden by bulging hills.

"What next?" inquired Hoot.

Pat raised his shoulders. "Beat it back, I guess." He thumbed his chin, considering. "Dakota figures we chickened out," he murmured. "If he slips through the fingers of that posse, and I'm gambling he'll do just that, it's likely he'll head for the hideaway. Maybe we'll round him up yet. You keep cases on the hideaway, but, for gosh sakes, stay out of sight. I'll hit for Adobe Wells and check with Bones Bailey when the posse rides in. Could be they'll corner Dakota, or chop him down. Then I'll head out to the Matthews place. You got any message, leave it with the girl."

"That'll sure be a pleasure!"

"And remember I already staked a claim."

"You sure don't give me a chance to forget," grinned Hoot.

They headed out of the mish-mash of hills to avoid the difficult terrain through which the herd had passed. When they hit the Basin flats the sun had begun to drop westward and shadows reached out from the slopes.

It was close upon sundown when Pat jogged into Adobe Wells. As usual, the clutter of adobes dumped on the baked plain seemed wrapped in lethargy. The broad stretch of Main Street was empty, save for the customary sprinkling of ponies tied outside The Wagon Wheel.

A girl stepped briskly out of the rambling store and the rays of the sinking sun glinted upon coppery tresses. Stepping up to the buckboard, she stood watching the clerk load.

"Howdy!" hailed Pat, jogging past. With a

smile, the girl raised a hand in greeting.

Acting upon impulse, the rider reined over, dismounted. There was something about Diane Bradley that stirred his pulse. Maybe, he thought, it was the taunting challenge of her green eyes, maybe the haughty angle of her small chin. While May Matthews was soothing, cuddly as a kitten, the Bradley girl was tempestuous, enveloped in a subtle aura of defiance. He just couldn't figure her as a dutiful helpmate, like May, broke to trot gently in harness. Like the broncs hitched to the Circle buckboard, she always seemed ready to take the bit in her teeth.

"I thought you'd left the Basin," she commented, her gaze straying over his dusty garb, then to the sweat-caked claybank.

"I've been cleaning up unfinished business," he returned shortly.

"Seems to keep you busy."

"You be surprised!"

"They say she's awfully pretty, and so demure." Her cool tones mocked him.

"What you yapping about?"

"Oh, quit acting innocent!" she returned crisply. "May Matthews, who else? She has Matt jumping through a hoop, too." Her shoulders raised with an abrupt gesture of resignation. "If the Bradleys and Harpers can find nothing else to clash over, there's always a woman."

"Quit kicking," he advised curtly. "You got Jules."

"Jules!" The girl straightened, a combative light in her green eyes. "Just what do you mean?"

"The way I heard it, you two are as good as hitched."

"Gossip — gossip!" she snapped. "Do you really think I'd marry that — breed?"

"Plenty gals would jump at the chance."

"Well count me out — way out," she threw back forcefully.

"Everything's loaded, Miss Bradley," said the clerk, and trundled his truck away. But the girl seemed in no haste to leave.

While he assured himself that he hadn't the slightest interest in whom she married, or when she married, he couldn't ignore a feeling of deep-seated relief at her vigorous denial of an attachment for Jules Garrott. "How's Bull?" he inquired, to make talk.

"Lying on his back," she replied, "and quite sick. His heart's bad. Dr. Lockwood insists that he rest. It's quite a problem making him conform."

It would be a heck of a bigger problem if the old moseyhorn were wise to the shenanigans of his son and his foreman, thought

Pat. His mouth twitched at the picture of Bull kicking both off the place.

"Is sickness so — funny?" snapped Diane.

"Heck — no!" he returned quickly.

"Any Bradley misfortune is grist to the Harper mill," she flamed. "Well, my father's a good man, and I love him." To Pat's amazement, tears glistened in her eyes.

Blinking, she swung away, hauled up onto the buckboard and snatched up the lines. At her impatient jerk the broncs came to sudden life. Dirt and pebbles scattered as their hoofs dug in and the buckboard shot off.

Pat stood watching the wagon whirl up street, jumping and jolting over chuckholes. It was a miracle the whole sheebang didn't overturn. That gal could fly into a tantrum quicker than hell could scorch a feather. Fellow who tied up with her would sure be hitched to a wildcat. But somehow the idea wasn't altogether displeasing.

Darkness had fallen when the posse dragged in — six weary, disgusted riders on gaunted ponies. Pat watched them file into Jorgenson's Livery and knew that Dakota, the old gray wolf, had slipped away.

As he sauntered along the plankwalk, the features of one, a yellow haired, red-faced rider, lingered in his mind. He'd seen that man before, someplace. Then, in a flash, he remembered. The yellow-haired man was the rider Jules had met outside the hotel the night the foreman propositioned him. Likely the hombre was a member of the rustling gang. And he'd ridden with the posse!

When he entered the law shack, Bones was opening his mail — and gnawing the ends of his sun-bleached mustache, a sign he was in no genial mood.

"So you tangled your spurs!" commented Pat.

Bones grunted and slit open an envelope.

"I lamped it" — Pat dropped onto a straightback chair — "from a high bench. Who got buck fever?"

"A cow-hocked, wall-eyed Cross puncher — name of Hawkins," rasped the deputy.

"How long Hawkins been riding for the Cross?"

"Six months, mebbe."

"He's yellow haired, ruddy faced?"

"Guess his face was red when I was through blistering his hide," growled Bones.

"He's a member of the rustling gang!"

The deputy swung around. "That gospel?" he demanded.

"I'd stake my life on it," said Pat. "He and Jules are like this." He raised a hand, two

106

fingers close together.

"So that shot warn't no accident," ruminated Bones.

"Hell, no! Hawkins was tipping off Dakota."

The lawman jerked erect, swept his battered Stetson off a peg with one hand and his gunbelt with the other. Buckling on the gunbelt as he moved, he headed for the livery. Pat dogged him.

In the big barn, several possemen were grooming their ponies. "Hawkins still around?" bawled Bones, stalking through the wide doorway.

"Pulled out ten minutes back," a man told him. "Seemed in one hell of a hurry."

"That's the last the Cross or you will see of Hawkins," Pat told the lawman.

"Or that Dakota hairpin," added Bones, with disgust.

"Maybe not," said Pat. "Hoot's keeping cases on the hideaway. If Dakota turns up, Hoot'll leave word at the Matthews' place. I'm riding out at sunup. I'll streak back if the lobo's around. Couldbe we'll corral him yet." Tentatively, he inquired: "Figure you've got enough on Matt or Jules to lay charges?"

"What have we got, except your word?" bit back the deputy.

"And the word of a Harper ain't worth a

damn in Big Basin," returned Pat tightly.

"You said it!" grunted the deputy.

Bones was right, reflected Pat. One man's unsupported hunch meant nothing. His father had been hanged for rustling. What would denunciation of Matt Bradley, the man who had hanged him, bring but a horse-laugh? Until one or more members of the gang could be rounded up and induced to spill their guts, Matt was safe.

When Pat rode into the tumbledown Matthews' place the following day, the sun was dropping behind the ragged silhouette of surrounding hills. Judd Mathews' sober-clad form was visible on the gallery, hunched over a solitaire layout. Seemed as though the T.B. victim was glued to that table, thought the rider.

May came to the door of the adobe, smiling welcome. It was a miracle how she retained her bubbling good humor, reflected Pat, isolated back in these sun-blasted hills and tied to a sullen invalid. A girl so innocent and sweet sure deserved better.

"Why, Pat," she cried, "it's so good to see you. We had another visitor — your friend Hoot."

He mounted the gallery and she advanced to meet him, eyes aglow. He had difficulty restraining an impulse to plant a kiss on her full red lips. "Hoot leave a message?" he inquired eagerly.

"Yes," she smiled, and pursed her lips, frowning prettily. "Now just what did he say? Oh, I remember: *Dakota's back. I'm keeping cases on the hideaway. Will ride back at sundown, tomorrow.*" She dimpled and bowed. "There it is, word for word, relayed by your faithful reporter."

"When did Hoot deliver it?"

"Last night, quite late."

Pat glanced westward. The sun had sunk out of sight and the western sky was suffused with deepening scarlet.

"Then he's due most any time," he commented. "Mind if I stick around?"

The girl glanced hesitantly at the back of the absorbed card player, then motioned Pat to follow her to the far end of the gallery. There she paused, swung lightly around to face him. "You're always welcome as far as I am concerned," she said softly. "You know that!"

"But your paw don't cotton to visitors," he grinned.

"He's a sick man!" she returned defensively. Then, pleading: "Why don't you go back to Amarillo, Pat? Your father is dead, nothing can change the past."

"I can get the man who framed Paw," he

returned tightly, "and to get Matt I've got to bust up this rustling gang."

"Haven't you considered that this rustling gang may bust you?" she retorted, an edge on her voice.

"There's more," he went on, dark eyes intent. "I'd kinda hate to leave you behind."

"You could always — write."

"Would you cut loose and join me?"

Eyes downcast, she impulsively grasped his arm. "Don't ask me to leave Dad," she whispered. "He needs me!"

"He won't live — forever!"

"Pat!" Her voice held shocked reproof.

"If he don't," the rider insisted relentlessly, "would you come then?"

"Maybe!" she returned quickly, planted a kiss upon his lips and whisked away. He watched her slip into the house and close the door.

Pulse speeding, he dropped onto a rocker and occupied himself making a cigarette. If it weren't for that sullen wreck silently laying out cards at the far end of the gallery, he thought, he'd gamble the girl would marry him tomorrow. She practically said so. And what sweeter helpmate could a man crave?

That Diane now, she'd likely prove as prickly as a porcupine. When this rustling gang was broken up and Matt got what was coming, he'd press May hard. Likely she was only playing hard to get.

Slowly, night closed in on the lonely spread. Stars pricked through the darkening heavens. Judd Matthews gathered his cards and entered the house, slamming the door behind him.

It was a sure thing the sunken-checked buzzard didn't fancy his company, thought Pat. The shaded windows of the adobe glowed with warm hospitality, but hospitality didn't seem part of Matthews makeup. Any other rancher would have invited a visitor inside. But Matthews was a city man and maybe they had different ideas in the cities. He acted like he was jealous, resented anyone paying attention to his girl. And May was sure scared of offending the stiff-necked bustard.

Time dragged. As a litter of cigarette butts grew around Pat, his restiveness increased. Sundown had long passed but still there was no sign of Hoot. With each passing moment the waiting rider's uneasiness grew. An unreasoning premonition that his pard had somehow tangled his rope, seized him. Finally, he could stand the strain of waiting no longer. He strode to his pony, mounted and headed out into the shadowed hills.

# XI

Bathed by wan moonlight, Pat pulled rein outside the hideaway, in the shadow of the rugged red wall. Ahead, a broad band of black marked the split in its face that gave way to the narrow valley. The claybank fiddle-footed nervously as the almost human, sobbing shriek of a mountain lion soughed through the solitudes.

Beyond that there was silence, a silence that enveloped the lone rider like a shroud. Pat still couldn't shake off his premonition of disaster, a deepset feeling that he'd never see Hoot alive again.

It was crazy to get riled up because Hoot had failed to return to the Matthews' place, he told himself. A dozen reasons might have kept his partner away. Maybe he was trailing Dakota; maybe he had been toled away, maybe his pony had broken a leg. There were endless "maybes."

He had said that Dakota was back, which

meant the rustler was in the hideaway. A conviction grew in Pat's mind that the answer to the problem was to be found in that hideaway.

He reined off, dropped down into a rocky draw. Here he tied the claybank to a squat greasewood and shucked his spurs. Legging up the draw, he headed for the split in the wall.

Ghosting into the fissure, he fingered ahead through darkness. Couldbe, he thought, ghosting through the gloom, the rustlers had cut out, and couldbe Dakota was lurking close ahead, waiting to cut him down when he emerged from the cut. Who could figure the wary old lobo?

Pale light showed ahead, marking the end of the gloomy alley. Dropping down on hands and knees, he began to crawl.

Braced for the blare of a gun, he crept out into moonlight. The narrow valley stretched ahead, apparently deserted. Nearby bulked the clutter of boulders where the lookout man usually took post. He was about to rise to his feet when the scent of burning tobacco hit his nostrils. He froze — someone was on watch. The rustlers had not abandoned the hideaway!

Again he dropped down, slithering toward the boulders until the misshapen rocks bulked massive around him, clothed with a sheen of moonlight.

Stretched out, he carefully slid his .45 out of leather. He found a chunk of rock, tossed it off to the right. When it dropped, the clatter was loud on the night.

Instantly, not six paces distant, a man's head and shoulders, crowned by a steeple-topped sombrero, bobbed up from behind a boulder.

"Reach!" barked Pat.

Startled, the lookout swerved toward him. Pat came up on one knee, sixgun leveled. "One peep and you're a dead duck," he grated.

Slowly, the man's hands raised. Pat came erect, moved forward. His Winchester lying on a rock before him, Sancho stood eying his captor with sagging jaw.

"Where's Hoot?" demanded Pat shortly.

Sancho's tongue ran over his thick lips. He was scared, registered Pat — scared stiff. "Spill it!" he snapped.

The vaquero gulped. "Senor Pat," he said earnestly, "Hoot was my fren'. I like heem. It was not my doing. I beg —"

"So Dakota beefed him!"

Sancho nodded mutely, then words spilled with a rush from his lips. "Dakota, he is wan crazy man. He scare me. He want to kill, only to kill. He say that Hoot was wan yellow double-crosser. He say you double-crosser and he keel you, too."

"Where's the lobo right now?"

The vaquero jerked his head in the direction of the camp. "He sleep, I theenk."

Pat stood silent, battling the shock of Hoot's death, weighing the Mexican's words. Sancho watched the leveled gun with distended eyes, as though it were a rattler poised to strike.

He should plug the Mex, thought Pat. That was the sensible thing to do, an eye for an eye, a tooth for a tooth. Maybe Sancho had cut down Hoot and was laying blame of Dakota to save his skin. But he couldn't rid himself of the feeling that Dakota had been the killer. Sancho had always proved a friendly cuss. He and Hoot had got along like two puppies on a warm brick. Likely he had been glad to see Hoot back. Dakota now, that hombre was a different breed of cat.

"Beat it!" he told the vaquero abruptly. "Head south and keep riding."

*"Gracias, senor!"* gasped Sancho, with relief.

In the dim light, Pat stood watching the vaquero lead his pony from beyond the rocks, saw the Mexican step into leather and vanish into the gloom of the cut.

*Now for Dakota!* Pat began legging toward the camp. He was passing a shadowed patch of trees when the crackle of breaking brush pulled him up short. He swung toward the trees, right hand darting to his gun butt. Staring through pale moonlight, he glimpsed movement.

Crouched, he eased closer, relaxed when he saw a coyote sneaking away with stealthy backward glance. Another was leaping, tearing at something suspended from a tree. As he approached, the remaining coyote crawled away after its mate.

A human form was hanging from a stout branch, the head twisted at a grotesque angle. Pat's intestines knotted — the garb was familiar! Stark horror in his eyes, he stepped up to the dangling body. Even in the uncertain light, he recognized Hoot Fuller's cold clay. The dead man's features were no pleasant sight — bloated, purpled with congested blood; the eyes staring, the mouth gaping.

His movements jerky, Pat brought out his jackknife and severed the taut rawhide rope from which the body was suspended. It dropped with a heavy, dead thud. For moments, he stood staring at the stiffening form, finding it hard to believe that Hoot,

116

still young, with his droll humor and un-questioned loyalty, was dead — hanged by a desperate, no-good renegade. No wonder, he thought bitterly, that Sancho was scared, fearful of retribution. He should have downed that lousy Mex.

He began to move out from the shadows of the scrub oak, heading for the camp. Still bemused by shock, he walked stiffly, like a sleepwalker. Forgetful of caution, he reached the screening chaparral clumped around the camp, and blundered through it. He stumbled over a wire, looped through the brush. Loose pebbles, in cans hung from the wire, jangled.

A gun bellowed and a slug whipped through the undergrowth. Pat dropped flat, shocked into alertness. Dakota never missed a bet, he thought. The crafty renegade figured he would likely be around, hunting Hoot, so had rigged trip wires to offset any chance of surprise attack.

Dakota's dry, rasping challenge came through the night: "Howdy, yellerbelly! I stretched your pard's neck and I'll hang your stinking hide up to dry, too."

Pat's somber mood had fled, leaving smoldering anger. One or the other of them, he vowed silently, would never leave that hideaway.

Silence followed Dakota's challenge. Pat kept his lips locked, just lay flattened. Then, cautiously, he began crawling through the brush, not toward the sound of Dakota's voice, but away from it, circling beyond the dark bulk of the cabin.

Every minute or so, he paused and listened. Mentally, he tried to figure Dakota's movements. Was the rustler stealthily stalking him through the brush, or was he waiting, on the defensive?

Likely he was forted up, behind cover, awaiting a chance to use his gun again.

Behind the cabin, Pat came to a stop on the fringe of the chaparral. Flattened, right hand latched onto his sixgun, he cautiously raised his head. Dim in the faint moonlight, he eyed the corral, the form of a pony botched beyond its rails. To his left, across a bare patch of ground, was botched the rock fireplace, nearby it a bedroll and a saddle.

The rider lay figuring his next move in the deadly cat-and-mouse game. It was a sure thing he had to kill or be killed; mercy was a quality unknown to Dakota. The rustler probably packed a Winchester. Odds were, too, that the rustler had rigged a whole system of trip wires to offset the chance of a surprise attack. He'd had time to prepare and he was fighting on his own ground.

Seemed the lobo held all the aces.

His only chance of survival was to out-smart the bustard. How?

From behind the corral came the whisper of the spring. The sound sparked an idea. He remembered thick brush clustered above the pool, twice the height of a man. That brush must be growing on some kind of a ledge. If he could gain the ledge unseen, the brush would cover him and he'd have the entire camp spread below. Not only would he have a bird's-eye view of Dakota's movements, but both corral and cabin would be within range of his .45.

Inch by inch, he began to slither across the bare stretch of ground that separated him from the corral, braced for the bark of a gun, the whiplash of a bullet. But no sound disturbed the serenity of the night as he eased ahead.

He gained the shelter of the corral and breathed more easily. Snaking along its side, he suddenly froze as the head of the pony drowsing beyond the rails came up, ears pricked. A whinny from the animal would be a clear giveaway.

The pony's head dropped and Pat softly exhaled pent-up breath. Creeping ahead again, he left the corral behind him and headed into a tangle of growth nurtured by the run-off from the spring. Thorns hooked his shirt and lacerated his skin as he wormed through it. A nest of enraged hornets couldn't be worse, he reflected, easing ahead. Abruptly, he found himself sinking into slimy mud and half-immersed in water that drained along the base of the cliff. Muddied, scratched, dripping water, he crawled out of the seepage onto firm ground, only to find himself tangled in another thorny disorder of vines festooned along the foot of the cliff. Fervently, he blessed a cottony mass of cloud that drifted over the moon, deepening the obscurity.

He struggled through to the cliff face, straightened, fingering its rugged surface. Easy climbing, he figured. The danger was that the eroding rock might crumble or break away under his weight. Just one fragment, clattering down, would betray him. Pinned against the cliff, he would make a prime target for Dakota's lead.

Well, he reflected, it was up to Lady Luck. He sure couldn't stay where he was and he wasn't going back. He just had to climb that cliff.

Fingering the rough surface, pressing against the crumbly indentations, he began to work upward, exploring ahead with crooked fingers, digging in with sharp boot toes.

Sprawled in the brush above the spring, on a ledge so narrow that had it been bare he would have rolled off, Pat peered through interlaced branches. His face and arms were bloodied by thorny lacerations. His garb was caked with drying mud and his fingertips raw from clawing sharp rock.

As daylight strengthened, the camp below became more clear. Nothing moved. Even the dun, standing hipshot in the pole corral, seemed asleep. Except for the pony, the place might have been deserted. It was hard to realize that a desperate man was crouched in the brush, or was worming his way through it, with but one thought — to kill.

Before, Dakota had been holding a winning hand. Now the odds were even — more than even. From his vantage point he could spot any movement in camp. Dakota couldn't quit. He'd need his saddlehorse to get out of the valley, and the dun was within easy reach of Pat's forty-five.

There was only one weakness in his position — the brush might hide him from sight, but a slug would whip through it. If Dakota guessed he was hidden there, the rustler could stay out of range of the .45 and shoot him so full of holes with the longer range

Winchester that he'd sink in brine. Once discovered, he was lost unless he tagged Dakota first. When he made his play it had to be good; he'd never have the chance to make another.

The fiery ball of the sun rimmed the hills to the east, slid into full view and poured heat into the valley. Quickly, the blasting rays became torture to the man stretched out on the narrow ledge. He dared not move and ease his limbs for fear that any shifting of the brush would betray his position. His mouth and throat felt as though he had been chewing ashes. The myriad of thorn scratches began to itch and burn. He would have given his right arm, he thought longingly, for just one sip of the water that splashed below.

He could do nothing but endure, wait, and watch.

As the day dragged toward noon, the heat built up, and the watcher lay parched, roasting, panting. Since dawn, there had been neither sound nor sight of Dakota. The only assurance that the rustler was still around was furnished by the dun hunched in the corral below. And that dun, Pat hoped, would toll Dakota to his death.

# XII

Growing weakness plagued the watcher. Fatigue, added to loss of sleep and the deadening effect of the burning sun, numbed his senses. Again and again, he found himself dozing off, to awake with a start, fearful that an involuntary movement had betrayed his position. It was past noon now, but still his opponent had given no sign of his presence. This was a battle of nerves, he reflected. Each waited for the other to betray his position. Sooner or later, one had to give in. They couldn't wait it out forever.

He had removed his hat and his eyes were sore and bloodshot from sunglare. Peering through some branches, he wondered just where Dakota had holed up. As though his cogitations had stirred action, the faint metallic clink of pebbles in a can reached his ears. It came from the chaparral behind the cabin. Seemed that Dakota, prowling, had tangled with one of his own wires.

Suddenly, to his amazement, the rustler stepped into full view, moving around an angle of the cabin. Plain in the sunlight, he stood with his back against the rough adobe wall of the cabin, Winchester cradled beneath his right arm, looking around him.

For a full minute he remained unmoving, the brim of a battered Stetson yanked down over his eyes, long jaw stubbled with sprouting beard — a somber, dust-grayed figure. Pat was reminded of a wolf testing the air for a strange scent. From beneath the hat, he knew the wary eyes were casting around, probing, suspicious.

Maybe twelve hours had passed since he last had evidence of Pat's presence. The rustler must have decided that the "yellowbelly" had pulled out. But some deep intuition, given to animals and men, still made him wary.

Apparently satisfied, he moved over to the rock fireplace, stood for a moment eying the blackened coffeepot and dead embers.

The dun snorted. He whirled, quick as a scared cat, throwing up the barrel of his rifle in automatic reaction. Then, relaxing, he propped the Winchester against a boulder, picked up a tin cup and sauntered toward the spring.

From the ledge above, not a dozen paces distant, Pat watched him bend, scoop up a cupful of water and drink avidly.

Quietly, the rider slipped his sixgun out of its holster. The click of the hammer, as he thumbed it back, must have reached the rustler's sharp ears. He froze abruptly, cup in hand, stood still as a statue. Then his head came up. He stared full into Pat's sun-blackened features and the muzzle of a .45.

"Howdy!" croaked Pat through parched lips.

Dakota galvanized into action. He hurled the cup and leaped for the shelter of the cliff. He was off the ground when the gun blared. The slug hammered into his left shoulder. He spun sideways, dropped. Water splashed as he came down in the pool. He scrambled out, water draining from his garb, and began rolling, snatching out his gun as his body corkscrewed.

Again, Pat's .45 bellowed. The twirling rustler doubled up, features twisted with pain as hot lead drilled into his belly.

He jerked to a sitting position, fired wildly. A third bullet slammed into his chest. The gun spilled from his fist. Arms and legs whipping, he flopped around, lifting dust.

Lips compressed, gun smoking, Pat watched from the ledge, remembering that a rattlesnake was liable to strike even when dying. But Dakota's fighting days were over. The threshing subsided. Limp, he lay on his back, a dark smear of blood draining sluggishly from his slack mouth. The body quivered once, then was still.

Pat came stiffly to his feet, plugged out his empties and slid fresh loads into the cylinders. He'd most fried on that ledge, he reflected. But Dakota would likely be finding it a mite hotter frying in hell!

He buried Hoot beneath the scrub oak, but left Dakota for the coyotes. Saddling the dead rustler's dun, he rode out of the hideaway and headed for the draw where he had left his own mount. Then, with the dun on a lead, he set out for the Matthews' place.

When he rode in, Judd Matthews was hunched over his eternal solitaire. May, fresh in a crisp cotton dress, sat on a rocker in the shade of the gallery, and a rider slacked in another rocker beside her. Pat's hackles rose when he recognized Matt Bradley.

He watered the ponies and tied them by the trough. As he approached, there was a bleakness about his taut features that drew the eyes of all three persons. Even the solitaire fan focused the visitor's muddy form, his scratched face.

May jumped to her feet with a startled cry. "What's wrong, Pat?" she called anxiously, advancing to meet him as he climbed the gallery steps. "You look awful!"

"Like he spent the night in a hog wallow," commented Matt from the rocker.

Pat ignored the derisive comment. He looked into the girl's anxious eyes and said tonelessly, "Hoot's dead. Guess I'm most tuckered out. Wal, I got Dakota."

"Dakota?"

He looked beyond her at Matt, dressed in a yellow silk shirt, scarlet bandanna, plated gunbelt. The Circle heir glared back with cold distaste. "Ask Bradley," he told the girl. "He rodded the sidewinder."

Matt came to his feet, an angry gleam in his green eyes. "There's no Dakota on the Circle payroll," he growled.

"Nope," barked Pat, "but how about your dogblasted rustling payroll?"

"You plumb loco?"

"Quit sidestepping!" gritted Pat. "You framed my paw; you been bleeding the Circle white, you been looting Basin herds."

"You're crazy as a coon!" declared the Circle scion. Flushed with anger, he moved toward his accuser, stiff-legged, fingering the butt of his holstered gun. "No one names me a lousy brand-blotcher."

The girl swung around, threw herself against Matt's burly form. "No!" she wailed. "Stop! Don't you see that Pat's not well. He doesn't know what he's saying."

With an impatient sweep of his left arm, Matt brushed the girl aside. She staggered against the gallery rail.

Pat stood waiting, right arm crooked. He'd never craved a showdown more.

But interference came from an unexpected source. Judd Matthews had risen from the card table. A few quick steps and he thrust between the two antagonists. His gaze, cold and expressionless, focused one, then the other. "Gentlemen," he said, in crisp, restrained accents, "take your fighting elsewhere. May and I came here to seek peace and rest. We want no blood spilled on our threshold." His voice hardened. "Go, both of you!"

Matt Bradley hesitated, then, with an angry snort, turned toward the steps. "Another time!" he threw at Pat.

"Any time suits me," bit back the rider.

While three pairs of eyes followed him, the Circle heir crossed the yard to his paint pony and mounted. Without a backward glance, he jogged away.

Judd Matthews turned to the fuming Pat.

"In future," he said shortly, "I'll thank you to keep your feuding away from here, and your person." He strode back to his card table, sank onto the chair, swept the pasteboards together and shuffled them deftly.

Pat glanced at the stricken face of the girl standing beside the gallery rail, lifted his shoulders and jingled off the gallery. Leaving Dakota's dun, he mounted the claybank and followed Matt, now halfway to the rim of the bowl. An impulse seized him to spur in pursuit, but fatigue leaded his limbs and the shock of Hoot's hanging still dulled his mind. Common sense told him that he was in poor shape to match guns with Bradley. As Matt had said — there would be another time.

When he reached the rim, the rider ahead had been swallowed by the tangle of hills. He had half expected to find the Circle heir waiting, braced for gunplay.

He turned in the saddle, still remembering the shock in May's eyes. Both father and daughter were standing in front of the house, watching. Couldn't blame Judd Matthews for giving him marching orders, he mused. They'd moved into the hills to seek peace. First they'd been plagued by a hanging and now he and Matt had threatened gunplay. They must sure figure the Harpers a wild bunch. Who didn't in Big Basin?

The claybank jogged on. Its rider's head jerked up and he checked his mount as sound of a gunshot punched through the air. It came from the south, the direction in which Matt would ride. While the echoes were still murmuring through the hills, another report followed. Matt was loosing lead to relieve his feelings, he decided. The Circle heir never could put a brake on his temper. Curious he didn't use his sixgun. Those reports came from a Winchester.

Night was beginning to cloak the Basin when he rode into Adobe Wells. Weary, he stabled the claybank and hit for his hotel. No longer than it took to shuck hat, boots and gunbelt he stretched out on the covers. In minutes he was asleep, the deep sleep of exhaustion.

Suddenly the bed seemed to rock. It quit, then rocked again. Pat struggled up from depths of fatigue with a foggy notion that a cyclone had swept down on the town. Then he became aware that bony fingers were digging into a shoulder, roughly shaking him awake. He sat up, yawning. Standing by the bed was the gaunt form of Bones Bailey, the deputy.

"Quit!" he mumbled, blinking into the

lawman's flinty eyes.

"Shake a leg!" rasped Bones. "Yank on them boots."

"What in creation's got into you?" protested Pat. Sleepily, he reached for his gunbelt, then saw that it was dangling from the deputy's left hand.

"What in creation got into *you*," barked Bones, "bushwhacking Matt Bradley? You're under arrest, and the charge is murder."

# XIII

Shocked into wakefulness, Pat stared incredulously at the lawman. "Bushwhacked?" he repeated.

"Drilled square between the shoulderblades — two slugs," barked Bones. "You should know, you were there."

The accused rider shook his head in denial. Recollection of the reports that had echoed through the hills after he had left the Matthews' place flowed into his mind. And he had thought Matt was loosing lead in a spat of temper!

"I heard the shots," he admitted slowly, "but I warn't around."

"You crave to dodge a hangrope," growled the deputy, "you got to do better than that." His tone brittled. "Git a wiggle on!"

Pat swung his legs off the bed and began pulling on his boots. "I'm clean!" he repeated. "I swear it on a stack of bibles. I never beefed Matt Bradley."

"Bottle it!" grunted Bones. "You'll have your say when we get to the office."

Pat followed the deputy down the stairway. Seemed his luck had turned sour, real sour. Not only had he lost his pard but now he was caught up in a murder charge. Someone had laid for the Circle heir, probably saw him head for the Matthews' place, then waited for him to take the return trail. Couldbe it was a disgruntled member of the rustling gang, couldbe a cowhand nursing a grudge. But the finger pointed straight at him — Pat Harper — and there was nothing he could do to prove his innocence. He'd had motive and opportunity. Everyone in the Basin knew that he and Matt Bradley had hated each other's guts.

The two trudged into the yellowing adobe that served as law shack. Pat dropped onto a chair, limp as a wet sack. The deputy dumped his prisoner's gunbelt onto a shelf and pulled up to the table. He found a stub of pencil and a writing pad and eyed the disconsolate rider frostily. "Now you kin make that statement," he rasped.

Tonelessly, Pat told of Hoot's hanging, his showdown with Dakota and his call at the Matthews' place, leading Dakota's pony. He and Matt had tangled and Judd Matthews had ordered them off the place. He had tailed Matt away from the ranch, lost sight of him, then heard two shots. He realized how it must all sound to the lawman. Bones must figure him guilty as hell, as would everyone who read that statement. Every word he had spoken pounded another nail into his coffin.

"Maybe the hombre who reported the killing had a hand in it," he suggested, with faint hope.

The deputy finished writing, then leaned back in his chair, stuffed the bowl of his corncob pipe and appraised the prisoner. "Sure," he replied, with faint derision, "a gal who never handled a gun in her life."

"May Matthews?"

Bones nodded. "According to the skirt, Matt was visiting when you rode in acting mighty queer. Seemed you'd just beefed the Dakota hairpin. You accused Matt of rodding the rustlers and both you hotheads go for your guns.

"Judd Matthews, her paw, stops the gunplay and gives you marching orders. Matt leaves, you follow." The deputy paused to fuel his pipe. "That gal says both she and her paw figured you two would shoot it out just as soon as you left the ranch behind. Sure enough, they heard two shots. She straddles Dakota's dun, which you left, and rides out. Matt's body's sprawled across the trail. She hightails back to the ranch. Her old man figures there's been a gunfight, steers her to town.

"I'm out there at sunup — and find it's a bushwhacking." He tapped the dottle out of his pipe. "Guess you were riled by Hoot Fuller's hanging; I kinda liked the colt myself. Then I guess you and Matt were fiddle-footing for the gal's favors, but bushwhacking" — he spat, with slow deliberation — "I never figure a Harper would sink as low as that."

"A Harper never did!" protested the prisoner. "I told a straight story and, I gamble, so did May. It looks bad, real bad, but" — his voice deepened — "I just ain't guilty, Bones."

"You'll never convince a jury," grunted the deputy. He rose. "Wal, I got to lock you up for a couple of days 'til a train leaves for the county seat. Empty your pockets!"

Relieved of jackknife, wallet and other personal belongings, the prisoner was conducted to another adobe, fifty paces behind the law shack.

Pat stepped into the shack and the gate clanged behind him. The outside door grated shut on dusty hinges and he was alone in a cell with another fellow prisoner.

135

His arrest and incarceration had been so sudden and unexpected that he had not yet fully absorbed the shock. Now comprehension of his situation hit him forcefully. He was alone, friendless and facing a murder charge. He would hang by the neck just as his father had done, for a crime he didn't commit.

Irked by bitter frustration, he latched onto the bars with both hands. Now he realized how a trapped animal must feel, caged beyond hope of freedom.

"What you jugged for?" The voice of the cowhand across the passage brought his head up.

"Murder!" he said shortly.

"Cripes!"

"For a killing I didn't commit," added Pat tersely.

"Sure," grinned Speck, and sat up. "They all say that. They claim I stole a saddle hoss. Hell, all I craved was my rights. Old Sam Durham out at the D-Bar owed me two months wages and wouldn't part with a dollar. So I straddled his best mare and hightailed."

"Wal, you didn't get far!"

"Likely all I'll get will be a stretch in the pen," grumbled the other. "Gawd, how I crave to bust out of this lousy joint!"

Deputy Sheriff Bailey didn't feel easy in his mind. Hunched at the table in the office, he meditated on the Bradley bushwhacking. Pat Harper's guilt seemed plain as the horn on a saddle. The Harpers and Bradleys had feuded as long as he could remember. Pat and Matt had tangled since they were knee-high, but he just couldn't figure Pat shooting a man in the back. It just didn't square with the rider's character.

The veteran lawman prided himself on being a keen judge of human nature. Matt he tagged as being wild with all his father's faults and none of his virtues. Pat had been a young hellion, too; the Harpers had a wild Irish strain in their blood, but all three boys had been square-shooters, and Pat was the steadiest of the bunch. He just was not the type to cut a man down from behind. A bushwhacker always showed a vicious streak. Pat was belligerent but never vicious. Nope, this killing was not in character.

Who, then, could have beefed Matt Bradley? If the Circle heir was tied up with rustlers, pondered Bones, it could have been most anyone. As a class, brand-blotchers were shifty, stealthy coyotes. Matt, with his overbearing ways, might have tangled with one, and the hombre had paid off.

Maybe he should poke around a mite. He rose, reached for his hat and hit for the livery. Shortly, he was heading eastward, toward the Aridos Hills.

The deputy stepped out of leather in a bouldery cut. He stuffed his pipe bowl and stood in the glaring sun, considering. This, he reflected, was the spot where he had found the body. Likely the bushwhacker had been stretched out on one of those ridges. Unhurriedly, he began to climb the nearest slope, angling across its loose surface. When he reached the crest he stood eying his pony, ground-hitched below, and decided that the bushwhacker would have located further back. Wintry eyes casting to right and left, his shadow shortened beside him, he moved through scrubby, knee-high brush.

The glint of sunlight upon metal caught his eye. With a grunt of satisfaction he stooped and picked up a brass cartridge case. *A .44,* he murmured, and stooped again to pick up another.

He located two indentations where the toes of the bushwhacker's boots had ground into the earth; more indentations where the elbows had been planted. Then he dropped the empty cases into a pocket of his vest and began to slide and skid down the slope.

Stepping into leather, he headed up the cut toward the Matthews' place. When he rode in, Judd Matthews was, as always, engrossed in a card game. The T.B. victim paid no attention to his visitor as the gaunt deputy swung out of leather. Bones sauntered over to the gallery rail, rested his arms upon it and relaxed, watching Matthews as he laid out cards, absorbed in his solitaire.

"Mister," drawled Bones after awhile, "I hate to bust in, but I've got some questions that call for answers."

The card played glanced up with quick impatience, glimpsed the metal star pinned to his visitor's vest, and smiled warmly. "I was wrapped up in the game," he explained. "There's nothing else to occupy what time I have."

"About this killing," said Bones. "I got the gal's version. It seemed straight. You folks lamp any other hombres around that day?"

"No!" replied Matthews decisively. "We get few visitors, and I'd prefer fewer."

"Matt Bradley let drop anything about trouble — with some other hombre?"

Matthews' sharp features creased into an amused smile. "Not to me! My daughter

139

does the entertaining." He raised his voice. "May!"

The girl hurried out of the adobe. At sight of Bones her features straightened. "Oh!" she exclaimed. "I do hope you didn't call to discuss that horrible murder."

"Guess I got no option, ma'am," said the deputy dryly.

"I told you everything I know. Who but Pat Harper could have shot poor Matt. They drew their guns right here. If Dad hadn't intervened there would have been blood shed on this gallery."

"Seems so!" agreed the deputy. "You folks keep any guns around?"

"Why, no," she smiled. "I wouldn't know one end of a gun from the other."

"How about you?" Bones turned to Judd Matthews who had gathered up his cards and was shuffling and reshuffling with obvious irritation.

"I'm afraid I'm more familiar with a pen than a gun," replied the invalid with a faint smile. "And, may I add, I have no desire to own or use one."

"Most folks in the Basin keep a shotgun — for coyotes."

"We're from the city," put in the girl, amusement in her gray eyes. "We're just not used to country customs."

140

"Wal," decided the deputy, "I reckon that's all. Seems like Harper plugged Bradley, but I got to check. Sorry to bother you folks." He lifted his old Stetson and turned toward his pony.

Back in Adobe Wells, he rode into the livery. He was stripping off his pony's gear when Swede Jorgenson stumped up.

"Too bad about Matt Bradley," said Swede, propping himself against a nearby stall. He shook his head dourly. "I'd never have figured Pat a bushwhacker."

"Don't seem much doubt," returned Bones, spreading his sweaty saddle blanket. "Pat keep his Winchester hereabouts?"

"Couldbe it's in the boot," said Swede, and stumped away. He came back with a rifle. Bones took the gun, levered a shell into the breech, sauntered to the wide doorway of the barn and loosed a shot skyward. The empty shell tinkled down as he ejected it. He picked up the brass case, eyed it intently.

"Prove anything?" inquired Swede, coming up behind him.

"Couldbe!" returned Bones.

# XIV

Confined in the adobe jail, Pat paced the floor. He and Speck, the young cowpoke, had little in common and they quickly ran out of talk. Toward sundown of the second day both were lying on their straw cots, sleeping, when the padlock securing the outer door rattled. Through deepening gloom, Pat saw Jules Garrott stride in, followed by a new deputy — a middle-aged man with a bulky middle, a star pinned to the vest of his store suit. He looked well fed, pompous. The gunbelt the stranger wore belonged to Pat.

"Can't give you more'n ten minutes," said the lawman loudly as he lit a stable lamp dangling from a peg beside the door and withdrew.

That sure was the greenest deputy he had ever come up against, decided the prisoner. The jasper needed his head examined — leaving a visitor alone with an accused murderer. When Bones wised up he'd throw forty fits.

Garrott jingled up to the bars of Pat's cell. The prisoner slid off his bench, wondering what in creation had brought the Circle foreman.

"So you salivated Matt!" commented Garrott, and Pat could have sworn that smug satisfaction smoldered in his dark eyes.

"You know different!" snapped the prisoner.

"Me!" It was plain that the burly foreman was taken aback.

"Heck, you had more to gain from his death than I had. You'll rod the gang and likely take over the Circle if Bull checks out."

Garrott swung around and darted a swift glance at the cowpoke, apparently sleeping in the cell across the passage.

"Quit bellering!" he growled. "You crave to make more trouble?" With a cold smile he added; "I ain't claiming to be heartbroke. Matt always was a pain in the arse. As for beefing the maverick, I never left the Circle the day he stopped them slugs — and I got plenty witnesses."

"Couldbe you ordered it!"

"Quit putting on an act!" barked the foreman with a touch of impatience. "Everyone's wise how it was between you two."

The prisoner realized the futility of argument. Whether the foreman was hurrahing him or not, he knew that everyone in the Basin felt the same way about his guilt. "You'll hang, sure as shooting," added Garrott.

"So you called to crow?"

"Nope," returned the other, "I figured on getting you out of here. We kin still use your gun."

Pat regarded the foreman's lantern-jawed features, his hard wary eyes, and wondered what was behind all this. Just what did Garrott know?

The foreman's voice broke into the prisoner's cogitations. "I got it figured thisaway. Matt tipped Bones Bailey about the herd — he sure craved to see you behind bars. Dakota was always as sullen as a sore-headed dog. I gamble he prodded you and Hoot in the hideaway and lead flew."

Pat nodded. It seemed that Garrott's suspicions lay elsewhere.

"So that doggoned Bradley cub scrambled the eggs," continued Garrott. "Wal, now we got a new deal."

"With you kingpin!" said the prisoner with little interest.

The foreman ignored his comment, threw

another quick glance toward the sleeping cowpoke, and lowered his voice. "First, we got to get you outa here. Bones been called away — a fracas out at the Window Sash. The hairpin he charged to keep cases on the hoosegow don't know dung from wild honey."

He slipped a stubby derringer from beneath his waistband and passed it between the bars. "I'll have a saddlehorse staked out behind this joint around midnight. When you hear me whistle, raise a ruckus, toll that two-bit deputy inside, grab his keys and beat it." His thin lips curved in a grin. "It'll be like taking candy from a kid."

Pat stuck the derringer inside his shirt. "Sounds good to me," he admitted.

"Hit for the hideaway," added Garrott.

The paunchy deputy came to the door. "Adios!" said the foreman, and dropped an eyelid.

Left alone, except for his fellow prisoner, Pat looked the gun over, slipped it into a pocket, and dropped down on his bench, pondering upon Garrott's unexpected visit.

Outside, night thickened. Time to put Garrott's plan to action.

Pat swung his legs off the cot, crossed to a corner of his cell and grabbed the metal slop bucket. He began pounding it against the bars.

Awakened by the din, the cowpoke jerked to a sitting position. "Quit the racket!" he yelled.

Vigorously Pat continued to pound away. The clamor, he thought would most wake the dead. The door swung open and the sleepy deputy stood on the threshold, uncertainly fingering the butt of his holstered gun. "Stop!" he shouted. "Stop, or I'll — I'll shoot."

Pat dropped the bucket, displaying the ugly little derringer latched in his right fist. It was lined on the deputy's bulging belt line. "Reach!" barked the prisoner.

Jaw slack, the deputy stood staring at the squat gun.

"Reach — or take a slug in the guts," Pat repeated. "There's one killing chalked up against me right now. I got nothing to lose."

Slowly, the plump man raised both arms. Relief flooded Pat; he had been scared the man would bolt.

"Gee willikens!" ejaculated the cowpoke, now an avid spectator. "A break!"

"Open this gate," directed Pat.

Unsteadily, fear in his eyes, the deputy moved forward. At the cell gate he yanked out a ring of keys. The gate rasped open.

With a surge of relief, the prisoner stepped out, jammed the muzzle of the leveled derringer into the lawman's belly. With his free hand, he slipped the buckle of the familiar gunbelt, swung it clear. Eying the quaking guard, he looped the belt around his own waist, securing it.

Snatching the keyring from the man's limp fingers, he shoved the deputy inside the cell, slammed the gate shut.

"Now me!" yelled the cowpoke.

Pat turned toward him. "You bust out and they corral you," he warned, "the judge will take it out of your hide."

"I want out!"

Pat shrugged, moved to the cell gate, and began trying keys in the lock. When the gate opened, the puncher pushed out, eager as a colt released from a stall, and rushed impetuously for the open jail door.

Pat grabbed a shoulder, checked him. "Listen," he said, "there's a saddlehorse tied out back. Fork it and hightail." He thrust the derringer into the other's hand.

"Ain't that your bronc?" objected Speck.

"Nope," Pat told him. "I got a claybank in the livery. I'm straddling that." He stepped to the doorway, cautiously poked his head out and surveyed, the surroundings. There was little to be seen in the starlight, beyond the vague bulk of the law shack and the blurred outlines of stores on either side. No one seemed to be around.

He turned to Speck standing eager at his elbow. "Beat it!" he said. "Good luck!"

"I'm sure thanking you, pard," returned the other fervently. "I was all set for a spell in Huntsville." He stepped outside, glanced quickly about him and ducked around the angle of the jail.

When the cowpoke vanished from sight, Pat darted a glance back into the jail. The deputy hunched forlornly on the bench of the cell, hands between his knees, fingers interlocked. All the fight had gone out of him, if he ever had any fight, thought Pat.

Pat's head jerked around as a Winchester spanged somewhere outside, its sharp report cutting through the night. The man in the cell gasped. Pat froze. Sounds of pony's hooves reached his ears, dying with distance.

Quick suspicion leaped into his mind. He ran out, circled the adobe. Just beyond the rear wall a dark form lay motionless, sprawled on the ground.

He dropped on his knees beside it, rolled the body over. In the starlight he gazed into Speck's features, slack in death. The cowpoke's worn blue shirt gaped open. Blood welled from a puckered hole just below his throat.

"High and center!" muttered Pat. "The poor bustard never knew what hit him."

Now the reason for Jules Garrott's solicitude became plain, as plain as though written in letters of fire. The foreman had tricked him, planned to toll him out of the jail and cut him down. The scheme had worked to the letter, except that Garrott hadn't figured another man would take Pat's place. Instead of a saddlehorse behind the adobe, the foreman had been waiting — waiting to blast the life out of him. And, but for a trick of fate, Garrott would have succeeded.

"The dirty yellow rattlesnake," growled Pat. Seething with anger, he came to his feet. Dim in the night, men were emerging from the alleys that knifed between stores, attracted by sound of the shot. In the jail, the penned deputy began yelling frantically.

# XV

The fugitive crouched, watching shadowy forms converge upon the jail. It was plain he had to make himself scarce, fast, before news of the break spread.

He began ghosting across the flat. Circling, and still unobserved, he came to the back of stores higher up street, ducked into the welcome gloom of an alley. Trusting to the darkness to hide his identity, he sauntered across street, angling for the bulk of the livery barn.

When he stepped through the broad doorway a pungent horsey odor hit his nostrils. He plucked a match from his hatband. Feeble light flared, enough to enable him to locate a stable lamp.

Touching light to the wick, he moved quickly down the stalls, hunting the claybank. He found it, led it out and began swiftly throwing on its gear. He was about to set a foot in the stirrup when the thought came that he would be a fugitive. He'd need food, water. Swede, he remembered, had always eaten at the livery in the old days. Likely, he still had the same habit.

Leading the pony, he moved up to the front of the barn, ducked into the tackroom. Inside, the stable lamp sent shadows dancing over the sleeping hostler's form. Airtights and other foodstuffs were stacked on shelves behind a small iron stove in the rear.

With Swede's snores on his ears, the fugitive poked around, found a gunnysack. Quickly, he began pitching supplies into the sack. Suddenly, he became aware that the snoring had ceased. He spun around. The bearded man was seated on the edge of his bunk, silently eying him.

"Don't pay no mind to me," said Swede. "I only own the stuff."

"Make out a bill!" returned Pat. "I'll pay later." He swung the swollen gunnysack over a shoulder.

"You got more gall than a wagonload of monkeys," grumbled Swede, but made no hostile move. "You bust out of the hoosegow?"

Pat nodded, standing on the threshold. "I raise a ruckus," asked Swede, "you'd salivate me, like you salivated that Bradley colt?"

"Like hell I would!" returned the fugitive

forcefully. "I'm no yellow bushwhacker!"

"Matt was a lousy cuss, but he deserved better."

"Tell that to the hombre who beefed him," threw back Pat. His voice hardened. "Dumb up, Swede!" With that, he slid through the doorway.

The hostler sat sleepily looking after him, then stretched out on the bunk again. Soon he began to snore.

Out on the runway, Pat secured the gunnysack behind the cantle, stepped into leather. In no apparent haste, he walked the pony outside. His quick glance up and down street registered no movement except around the saloon. He raised the claybank's reins and jogged out of town.

Main Street dropped behind. The fugitive passed outlying shacks, hit the open plain and headed for the Aridos Hills.

Dawn found him bellied down amid the broken rock of a bare ridge on the flanks of the Aridos Hills. Nearby, in a ravine, the claybank was tied in the shade.

Below, the fugitive eyed waves of rolling hills, seamed with cowpaths. And set among them, dwarfed by distance, was the Circle B. A black thread of smoke from its cookhouse rose up into the still air. Rays of the rising sun glinted upon the motionless blades of a windmill.

In the distance, the Bradley spread looked like a small town, with a long, one-story, rock-and-adobe ranchhouse. A bunkhouse of the same construction, with a lean-to cookshack, sat opposite. Around were grouped barns, blacksmith shop, wagon shed and corrals. Ponies grazed in a wire-fenced pasture. The yard seemed alive with scurrying ants.

Bull's crew saddling up for the day's ride, thought Pat, and leveled the spyglass he had swiped from Dakota's saddlebag. He adjusted the telescope until buildings and men seemed to leap close, within a stone's throw. He was seeking Jules Garrott, for there was an account to be balanced. He eyed the flurry around a corral as the Circle punchers roped their mounts, led them out and saddled up. He watched them jog away, two by two, to scatter over the range and handle their daily chores.

But there was no sign of Garrott's burly form. Finally, the fugitive lowered his spyglass. He could wait, he reflected. There was chuck enough in that gunnysack to keep him going for a week. If Bones took after him with a posse, he'd duck into the chaos of the Aridos Hills. They'd never comb through those hills in a lifetime.

Sooner or later Garrott would leave the ranch, alone, and he'd brace the bustard. It would be a pleasure to feed the coyote a pill he'd likely not digest!

Toward noon, a flutter of white in the Circle yard caught the fugitive's eye. Again he adjusted the telescope, watched Diane Bradley in white shirtwaist and dark pants, ride out of the yard and into the hills, heading directly toward him. Idly, he lay watching the rider as she bobbed in and out of sight, beating up into the Aridos.

Diane always did have a yen to ride on her lonesome, he reflected. In the old days he occasionally met her, clad in overalls, braided hair dangling down her back like a pigtail, wandering through the hills astride an old cowpony. Usually, they'd join forces for awhile, but sooner or later he'd yield to temptation — yank her pigtail, or slyly dig her mount in the barrel with a rowel, and race off. Then she'd spur after him, green eyes sparking, quirt swinging. And she hadn't been backward in using that quirt! Put a Harper and a Bradley together and they always struck fire!

Engrossed with his thoughts, he failed to notice another rider pull away from the spread, trailing Diane Bradley. Suddenly a smudge of dust drifting in rear of the lone girl aroused his curiosity. He examined it with the spyglass and his nerves tightened. The rider who raised it was Jules Garrott!

Absorbed, Pat watched the two, switching from one to the other. Garrott was making no effort to close in on the girl and she apparently had no suspicion that she was being trailed. She pulled into a draw. Dismounting, she looped her reins around a tree trunk and stretched out on her back, lazily relaxed.

When Garrott approached the draw, Pat decided it was time to get down there. Snapping the spyglass shut, he wriggled back off the skyline and headed for his pony.

He heard the pair before he sighted them — Garrott's low-voiced cursing, the panting breath of the girl, the scuffle of feet. He broke out of the brush and checked his mount, dumbfounded.

The burly foreman and the girl were locked together in a swirling, scuffling struggle. Garrott had one of her arms pinned and was endeavoring to grasp the other.

A weal gleamed red across the foreman's swarthy features where she'd laid the lash, and blood beaded from scratches that crisscrossed his cheeks. Writhing, kicking and clawing like a wildcat, the coppery-haired Diane battled her snarling opponent. Her white shirtwaist had been ripped from her shoulders and dangled in ragged strips from her waist; her gleaming hair streamed over her face and shoulders in tangled disorder.

"Quit!" barked Pat, and swung out of leather.

It was plain that his approach had been unnoticed by the two. Garrott loosed his grip on the girl and whirled around. At sight of the fugitive his jaw dropped. Stiff with surprise, he stood gaping, as though suddenly confronted with a ghost. Then he yelped, "Harper!"

"Yep!" mocked the rider. "You figured me dead behind the jail, you lousy, yellow-bellied Siwash." He laid a hand on the butt of his gun. "I figure leaving you dead in this draw."

"Listen," begged the breed, shrinking back and raising both hands as though to fend off lead, "I never —"

"Quit sidestepping!" snapped Pat. "Go for your gun!"

Clutching the remains of her shirtwaist against her heaving breasts, the girl stepped between them. "Hasn't there been enough killing?" she panted, her green eyes glowing sparks of fire focusing one, then the other. "A cowardly murderer and a dirty rapist!" she taunted. "Once we had men in the Basin."

"I didn't plug Matt!" asserted Pat stonily. He glowered at the foreman. "Maybe the bushwhacker's right there!"

"That — animal," she retorted, swinging around to face Garrott, "never left the ranch the day Matt was killed. Why don't you quit lying, Pat Harper?"

"I suppose Matt was lily-white," he retorted hotly. "You forgot — he hanged my paw."

"For rustling Circle beef!"

"Paw never lamped them steers! Matt framed him."

"So you'd blacken a dead man's name to excuse murder," she flung back scornfully.

Preoccupied with this new dispute, Pat had forgotten Garrott. He suddenly realized that, covered by the girl's form, the foreman had edged away toward his pony.

"Garrott!" he yelled. "There's a payoff due. You ain't sliding out." But the other was leaping for the back of his mount, sweeping up the reins. The animal leaped forward, plunging through the chaparral. Pat watched impotently, gun half drawn, scared to shoot for fear of hitting the girl.

"Why don't you shoot the brute in the back?" she mocked. "That's your style."

The fugitive said nothing. Fuming with frustration, he dropped the .45 back into leather.

Sound of repressed sobbing pulled his eyes to the girl. Head bowed, white shoulders bare, face hidden by the tumble of copper hair, she stood weeping uncontrollably.

He stepped up to her, stood eying the quivering form. Then, awkwardly, he reached out and touched her bent head, striving to express sympathy.

She recoiled as though from a striking snake. "Don't touch me!" she shrilled hysterically. "There's blood on your hands."

Cold anger surged through the fugitive. Roughly, he grabbed her bare shoulders, his fingers sinking into the soft flesh. "Listen!" he grated, shaking her. "I had no use for Matt, but I didn't kill him. Calling me a liar don't make me a liar. I still figure that yellow-gutted Garrott ordered the killing. Matt was kingpin of a gang that rustled Basin stock. The breed was his right bower. Maybe Garrott craved to take over."

"Do you have to blacken Matt's name?" she threw back brokenly. Her voice was steadier now and the hysteria had strained out of it.

"I know it hurts," he returned bleakly, "but it's gospel."

"It's a lie!" she declared violently.

"Ask Bones Bailey," he returned, a weariness in his voice. "I joined the gang to get the lowdown. Bones knows that, too."

Of a sudden, her arms were around his neck and she was clinging to him desperately as another storm of weeping seized her. "Oh Pat," she sobbed, "I don't know who or what to believe. Matt's dead, Dad's dying. I'm all alone. I'm so confused, so scared."

He held her shaking body tightly, wordlessly stroking her hair, striving to soothe her. She drew a deep breath, pulled away, knuckling tears with the back of a hand.

"What a crybaby I turned out to be," she said wanly.

"Things will straighten out," he assured her earnestly. "Kick Garrott out and get a foreman you can trust."

"I can't," she said tonelessly. "That beast would just laugh if I tried to fire him. Dad gave him full charge. Dad still thinks I'm a harem-scarem kid."

"What about — today?"

"Dad's too far gone to understand."

"Them scratches on Garrott's ugly map would take plenty of explaining."

For no good reason they both laughed.

"Weren't you in jail?" she asked curiously.

"I broke out — last night. Right now I'm hunting the jasper who beefed Matt. Ain't no other way I can clear myself." He eyed her appealingly. "Now call me a liar again!"

"I believe you, Pat," she said quietly and began gathering the ripped shirtwaist, trying to cover her breasts. "I must look like a shameless hag."

"Wal, maybe like a tornado struck you," he admitted with a grin. He turned and strode up to his mount, loosed a rolled slicker from behind the cantle, shook it out. Then he draped it over the girl's shoulders like a cloak. "Maybe that'll serve for now," he said. "You pack a gun?"

"No," she returned tightly, "but I will from now on."

"Wal, I got to make tracks," he said regretfully. "Odds are Bones is trailing me with a posse, and that Garrott lobo is liable to come helling back with a bunch of Circle hands."

"Goodbye." Her tone had a softness he'd never heard before. "And, Pat — I don't hate you anymore."

"You never had cause to before," he retorted gruffly. With that, he turned away and hurried to his pony.

The girl's eyes followed him. When he raised a hand and rode away, she sighed and moved somberly to her own mount.

# XVI

The sun was high now, searing the slopes. For no good reason, as the fugitive bored deeper into the hills, he lifted his gun out of the holster, swung out the cylinder to examine the loads. A gasp escaped him — the .45 was empty! There was not a solitary bean on the wheel.

Abruptly, he reined the claybank to a halt, sat blankly eying the empty gun. Lady Luck had sure been riding on his tail, he thought. If Garrott had taken up his challenge in the draw, he would now be buzzard bait. And if he hadn't checked that cylinder through sheer chance he would sure have taken the big jump next time he matched cutters. Howcome the gun was empty?

A likely reason entered his mind. Bones, the deputy, was a methodical old cuss. He'd abstract the shells for safety's sake after impounding the gun. When he had been called away, his substitute had seen the gunbelt lying on the office shelf and buckled it on, neglecting to check the loads in the gun. The fugitive chuckled, reflecting on his run of luck, then fingered the loops of his gunbelt. Chilly dismay fastened upon him. Most of the loops were slack. In the rush of events before his arrest he had overlooked refilling them. His questing fingers found only four shells.

Slipping the loads into the chambers, he snapped the cylinder into place and dropped the .45 back into leather. Lips tight, he considered his predicament. Ammunition was as vital as food. Without shells he was virtually helpless. There seemed to be only one answer — come nightfall he'd have to backtrack to town, brace Jorgenson again and gamble on the hostler's goodwill to refill those empty loops. It was taking a long chance, he mused, but he had no option. Without shells, he was as helpless as a hamstrung horse.

It was near midnight when he ghosted into Adobe Wells. Main Street, silvered by moonlight, was as placid as a shadowed stream. He drifted up street. Ahead, ponies tied to the rail outside The Wagon Wheel showed plain in yellow shafts of light slanting from the saloon windows. The plankwalks were gloomy canyons of silence.

He wheeled into the dark cavern of the livery barn, stepped down outside the closed door of the tackroom. When he eased the door open, Jorgenson's snores came through the darkness. He scratched a match and touched it to the wick of a stable lamp set on the table. Yawning and snorting, the liveryman came awake. His legs swung off the bunk and he sat blinking at the intruder. "You again!" he ejaculated.

"I need shells," returned the fugitive curtly. ".45 shells!"

The Swede sat tugging uncertainly at his beard. "Hell," he grumbled, "why you got to plague me? Bones'll nail me for helping an escaped prisoner and I'll likely go to the pen."

"I need shells," persisted Pat. "I'm most skunked."

"Ain't got nothing but 50–50's," declared the bearded man. "Never owned nothing but that old Sharps." He nodded at a gun propped in a corner.

"Swede!" entreated the fugitive. "I'm in a tight. You're known around town — mosey down street and beg or borrow a few shells."

"At this time of night!" expostulated Jorgenson. "You loco?"

Both stiffened at the sound of a horse's hooves rattling the loose planks of the runway. Pat reached and lowered the lamp wick. The hostler rose and stumped to the closed door.

"No shenanigans!" warned Pat. "I still got four beans on the wheel."

Jorgenson grunted, eased the door open a mite and peered out. Standing behind him, every nerve taut as a fiddlestring, Pat heard sounds of a rider unsaddling down the barn. After awhile, planks again rattled. Jorgenson quietly closed the door and the two stood listening in the dim light, their ears following the rider by his footsteps as he moved up the barn. They heard the stranger pause outside, move on again, more briskly. His footsteps died away. Pat released his breath.

Jorgenson swung toward him. "Beat it!" he urged. "If that hombre lamped your brand you're a dead duck."

"It's dark outside," objected Pat with more confidence than he felt. "Bones around?"

"Nope, he's still out of town."

"Then what I got to sweat about?"

"A lynching!" returned Swede grimly. "The boys feel bad about Matt Bradley. Talk is that you downed him to even up for your paw." His voice brittled with irritation. "Git! You're more nuisance than the itch." He paused at sound of shouting up street.

"Vamoose!" he barked with real concern. "I gamble that jasper knew the claybank was yours and wised 'em up."

The fugitive needed no further urging. The shouting was gaining in volume and drawing closer. Three quick strides and he was through the doorway. He swung into the saddle and reined the claybank around. When horse and rider issued from the barn, Pat's head swerved as he made swift survey of the street.

From the direction of the saloon, men were blobbed back, hurrying toward him. "That's the lobo!" yelled one. A gun blared. More gunshots shattered the quiet. Involuntarily, the rider ducked as a slug whipped past an ear. From beneath the canopy of the opposite plankwalk a man jumped out, waving a hand iron, racing to intercept him. The claybank, stretching out into a gallop, hurtled at him. Triggering as he moved, the man, almost under the pony's outstretched muzzle, jumped frantically aside. The bullet droned high, but the powder flash blinded Pat and scorched his shirt.

Spooked, the claybank rose high on its hind legs, forefeet flailing. Striving to stick to the saddle and fend off the attacker who had latched onto his right leg, Pat pounded the clinging man with his gun barrel. But the other hung on like a leech.

Desperately, Pat strove to break free. Other forms loomed around. Hands reached out of the haze. He was hauled out of leather and the .45 twisted out of his grasp. Enveloped in a flurry of dust, he fought to break free. In the pale moonlight, they swayed over the ruts, a kicking, punching, hard-breathing tangle of humanity. In their midst, the fugitive was conscious of nothing but the press of bodies and the slogging impact of blows as he fought blindly with fists and boots. Something hard and heavy slammed down on the back of his head — the whole scene spun around him like a dizzy fantango. He sagged, dropped, as consciousness left him.

The fugitive came out of blank oblivion to find himself in what seemed to be an inferno, an inferno of sound. As understanding seeped back into his aching head he saw that he was roped to a chair in The Wagon Wheel. Around him surged a press of men, yammering and drinking. Beside him stood Ace Ackerman. As always, the saloon man looked as neat as though freshly out of a bandbox, dark suit neatly pressed and white linen immaculate. And he wore his usual mask of smooth affability.

It was apparent to the prisoner that many

of the men elbowing around were drunk — very drunk. All appeared to be in a high state of excitement; the air crackled with oaths, yells and loud-voiced talk. A puncher with yellow hair, sun-scorched features and a hawkish beak of a nose began rapping the bar with a barrel of his sixgun. *Hawkins!* The rustler who rode for the Cross, then joined the posse and tipped Dakota off.

The yellow-haired man continued to rap until the babble stilled. His voice rasped into the bewildered prisoner's ears. "Wal, we cornered the sidewinder who bushwhacked Matt Bradley. Now what we going to do about it?"

"String up the bustard!" yelled a patron.

"I suggest," put in Ace in careful, precise accents, "that Harper be handed over to the law. A jury should decide his fate." His lips continued to move but his further words were drowned by derisive yells.

Again the yellow-haired rider rapped for silence. When the outcry ceased, he roared, "Hogwash! The law had him and he busted out. We got him and we sure ain't loosing the varmint. He's guilty, guilty as hell. Who's for saving the law a chore?" The saloon vibrated to a storm of yelling.

Wrists roped behind him and ankles lashed to the legs of the chair, the prisoner, still stupefied, stared around and found it hard to convince himself that this was not all a fantastic nightmare. But his gaze lit upon the crush of jostling men, mostly bleary-eyed and features flushed with liquor. Realization of the insane ferocity of a crazed mob brought a chilled hopelessness. This was a wolf pack, swayed only by passion; a many-headed monster whose only desire was to kill.

His intestines balled into an icy knot as conviction seized him that he could expect neither mercy nor justice here. He was doomed, doomed as his father had been for crimes he had not committed. Mentally, he damned his tragic recklessness in riding back to Adobe Wells.

Another hoarse voice broke out, thick with passion: "Let's get on with it!" A roar of approval greeted the words.

With dawn, thought the prisoner numbly, these men would be sober, decent citizens; now they were raging brutes. He cleared his throat, raised his voice in appeal for a fair hearing, but his words were drowned in the turmoil.

Someone had brought in a coiled rope and handed it to the yellow-haired puncher who elbowed through the press of men toward the prisoner. He gained the side of the tied man and stood fashioning a noose.

With leaden hopelessness, the prisoner resigned himself to his fate. With Bones away, no man could check this frenzied mob. He looked up, met the hard gaze of Hawkins. This hombre at least was sober, cold sober.

"You're hanging the wrong man," he asserted.

"The boys got different ideas," returned the other indifferently and dropped the loop over the prisoner's head. He tightened it with a careless jerk that brought an agonized gasp from the bound victim. With no haste, men pushing and surging around, Hawkins brought out a jackknife, severed the rope that secured the prisoner's legs to the chair, snapped the blade shut and jerked the victim to his feet.

As though leading a roped calf, he thrust between men searching for a convenient beam. He checked, climbed a table, tossed the length of rope over one of the sturdy crossbeams that served as support for the roof. Jumping down, he hauled in slack until the prisoner, chin raised upward, was stretched to full length by the rawhide biting into his throat.

"Lay aholt!" directed the executioner and tossed the rope carelessly into the press of men. A score of eager hands reached to grasp it.

Lips locked, Pat awaited the end. A brittle silence now held the men crowding around him. Through the quiet, Ace's precise tones flowed to his ears, again protesting the hanging. A growling chorus silenced the saloon man.

The rope tightened, closing on the victim's neck like a steel clamp. His body left the floor, the thunder of congested blood roared in his ears, his legs whipped wildly in the throes of strangulation.

# XVII

With morbid fascination, every eye in the saloon focused the strangling form jerking grotesquely at the end of the rope. So intent was their regard that not a head turned when the batwings banged back and two men hurtled through. Foremost was the trailstained form of Bones, the deputy. Behind him stumped the bearded Swede, nursing his heavy Sharps.

Bones rammed through the engrossed spectators like a pile-driver, spilling men to right and left. Rushing up to the convulsively kicking form, he snatched a knife and slashed the straining rope. The twitching body fell with a flat thud, inert as a sack of wheat. Bones dropped on his knees beside it, loosened the noose and threw it aside. No one interfered; no one made a move.

The victim lay slack, features suffused with blood, mouth gaping. A quiver went through his frame, his chest began to rise and fall with quick spasms, his breathing grew deeper as he sucked air into his starved lungs.

The deputy came to his feet and stood, thumbs hooked in his gunbelt, icy-blue eyes sweeping over the men bunched around. "Just a pack of lowdown coyotes," he barked in his harsh voice. "A gang of dirty lynchers! If I had the cells I'd jug every last one of you." He focused the saloon man, standing by the bar. "Howcome you stomached a ganging in your saloon, Ace?"

Ackerman spread smooth hands. "I had no choice," he explained suavely. "I registered protest, but —" his shoulders raised.

"Harper's a killer!" put in a townsman defensively.

"And that gives you the right to hang him!" barked the deputy. "Who in thunder appointed you judge and jury, Tom Amos?" Again his angry glance speared the suddenly sobered men thronging the floor. "I should book every hombre in this saloon for attempted murder — maybe I will!"

Boots shuffled as patrons began to move furtively toward the batwings. Their crazed frenzy had evaporated and all the elation had drained out of them. Their features bore the hangdog aspect of a store clerk caught dipping greedy fingers into his employer's cash box. It was plain they fervently wished themselves elsewhere. The batwings swung as men slipped outside, and among the first to go was the yellow-haired puncher.

The victim came to a sitting position, staring around with dazed eyes. Slowly, he levered to his feet, stood swaying on rubbery legs, fingering the red weal around his neck where the rawhide rope had bitten in. "Thanks, Bones!" he croaked. "Figured I was due to shake hands with St. Peter."

The apron poured a stiff shot of bourbon, handed it across the bar to his boss. Ace threaded between silent men, handed the drink to Pat. The rider emptied the glass with a succession of short, gasping gulps — his throat felt as though it had been cut.

He glimpsed himself in the backbar mirror and recoiled at the spectacle — dried blood matted his hair and his swollen features were streaked with sweat and dirt. His shirt had been completely ripped off, revealing a torso mottled with yellow-black bruises collected in the street fight. The mark of the rope impressed upon his neck stood out like a rusty collar. He turned to the deputy. "Gawd, I look even worse than I feel." His voice came out as a hoarse whisper.

Men were crowding the batwings now,

eager to get out of sight of Bones.

"You in shape to leg it over to the office?" the lawman asked Pat.

"Sure!" whispered the rider.

Side by side, the two plowed through the dust of the wide street. Vague in the moonlight, men clustered along the plankwalks in low-talking groups. Lighted windows winked out of the night — the whole town was awake and stirring uneasily.

The prisoner followed Bones into the law shack. The deputy touched a match to the lamp, jerked down the shades over two dusty windows and dropped into a chair by the plank table. He motioned the battered Pat to another seat, and brought out his corncob pipe. "Wal," he grunted, "you figure you raised enough hell?"

"Me!" expostulated the prisoner. His voice still issued as a husky croak. "Did I stage that lynching bee?"

"You made a break — and triggered the fracas."

"You figure I craved to stick around and hang for a doggone bushwhacking — when I'm as innocent as a newborn calf?"

"You most hanged anyway," commented the deputy with grim humor. He scratched a match and lit his pipe. "If you'd had a mite more patience you'd have been cleared of the killing."

"Cleared! You got the bushwhacker?" Pat's voice raised with excitement, then he fingered his throat ruefully.

"Nope!" admitted Bones. "But them .44 slugs never come from your Winchester." He groped in a pocket of his vest, brought out three brass shell cases, handed them to Pat. "Look 'em over," he invited.

The prisoner examined the empties with interest. Each was that of a .44 shell. Two, he decided, had been fired by the same rifle, but not the third.

He dropped the shells back into the deputy's palm. "They're from two guns," he said.

Bones nodded. "Them two with the firing pin dents off center came from the bushwhack gun. The other was from yourn."

"Which clears me!" exclaimed Pat. Impulsively, he jumped to his feet. "Bones, you old horntoad, you look like Santa Claus to me." He latched onto one of the deputy's bony hands, pumped it fervently, then inquired, "You checked Garrott's gun?"

"Garrott's clean!"

Pat remembered Diane's assertion that the foreman hadn't left the Circle B the day of the killing. But, somehow, he wasn't convinced. Garrott, he thought, was as crafty as

176

a coyote. The foreman had most tolled him into hot lead when he tricked him into making a break. Guns could be switched.

"Who you figure then?" he inquired, bottling his suspicions.

Bones' thin shoulders raised. "Your guess is as good as mine," he confessed. The deputy lapsed into silence, puffing his pipe, deepsunk in thought. He head jerked up. "Hawkins figure in your hanging?"

Pat remembered the yellow-haired puncher who had taken charge. "That dog-goned rustler?" he returned tightly. "You bet your life he figured. Ran the show! I swear he was cold sober, too."

"H'm," mused the deputy, then switched the subject. "Listen," he said, "you slide out of town and bury yourself in the Aridos Hills for awhile. If the hombre who downed Bradley gits a notion I'm hunting a Winchester, he'll ditch the gun pronto, figuring it may hang him. I need time to mosey around."

"What'll folks say — you loosing me?"

"Folks'll figure you caged in the hoose-gow." The deputy rose, tapped out his pipe. "I'll lend you a shirt and you kin wash up out back. Right now you look like the tail-end of a misspent night."

"How about my pony?" asked Pat.

Bones fingered his chin. "Right now it's in the livery," he said, "and it better stay there. I'll have Swede slip you a bronc. The square-head will button up."

Bones' lanky form tossed Pat a trampled Stetson. "I'll dig out a shirt," he said.

"And a few .45 shells," added Pat.

"You short?"

"That's what brought me to town," confessed the rider with a wry grin, "and almost strung me up."

When the two moved out back again a saddlehorse stood in the shadows. "Now lay low," cautioned the deputy. "No grandstand plays. Leave this murder to me. Remember the gent who got Bradley could have a yen to get you."

"Sure glad to oblige," Pat assured him. "I've sure had a bellyful of trouble."

He walked the pony along the rear of stores fronting Main Street, past deserted loading platforms and outhouses. Dawn was close now and faint red stained the horizon to the east, but the town had apparently settled down to sleep again.

Taking no chances, Pat angled away from Main Street, easing the pony through gray obscurity. When he hit the open plain he raised his mount to a trot. Crossing the swales, through a vast spiderweb of shadow, he broke open the package of .45 shells Bones had given him, loaded his .45 and filled the loops of his gunbelt. Ahead, rays of the rising sun touched the tips of the Aridos Hills.

It was full daylight when the chaos of ravine and canyon closed around the rider. His thoughts went to May Matthews, soft-eyed and sympathetic, confined to a secluded ranch with an old invalid. May, he reflected, was one of the few real friends he had in the Basin. She welcomed visitors to break her dreary days. It would do no harm if he drifted their way. The girl would sure be happy to hear he was cleared of Matt's killing.

When the gelding breasted the rim of the shallow bowl deep in the hills and the weathered clutter of buildings he had once called home came into view, the rider's glance fell upon Judd Matthews' form on the gallery bent over the card table. That hombre sure got a bellyful of cards!

Riding closer, he tightened his bandanna to hide the rope mark around his throat. When he jogged up to the adobe, the T.B. victim's glance raised for a brief glance, remained rigid. Astonishment impressed upon his sharp features, the invalid stared incredulously.

"Howdy!" croaked the visitor, and swung out of leather.

The card player nodded slowly, seemed about to speak, compressed his thin lips and returned to his game. Pat grinned, enjoying Matthews' puzzlement. Hoarsely, he hailed the house.

May, desirable as ever, darted out, checked suddenly at sight of her visitor. For moments she stood as though frozen, eyes distended with surprise.

"It's me," grinned the rider. "Pat Harper, in person."

"You were — in jail," she faltered.

"Not no more," he chuckled. "Bones kicked me out."

With an effort, it seemed to Pat, the girl smiled, though he could have sworn that something akin to fear flickered in her gray eyes. "I'm so glad!" she faltered, and advanced to meet him.

"Say," he chided, "you don't have to act thataway. Bones cleared me of Matt's killing. The slugs that took him never came from my gun." Still doubtful, she darted a quick glance at her father, engrossed in his cards, then laughed a trifle breathlessly. "Tell me about it!" she urged.

"Ain't much to tell. It just wasn't my .44 that took Matt."

"How would the deputy know?"

"A city gal wouldn't understand," he returned indulgently. "Ain't it enough that I'm free as a bird?"

"Of course!" Somehow, her tone lacked conviction, but she grasped his arm, forced a smile and steered him onto the gallery. He dropped onto a rocker. The gal sat close by and confided. "I was so unhappy! There just didn't seem to be any doubt but that you shot poor Matt. Remember how you two argued?"

"You ain't the only one who felt that way," he admitted soberly, and thought of the lynch mob. "Wal, you know different now."

He rolled a smoke, watching the girl quietly, conscious of an atmosphere of constraint. It was apparent that doubt still lingered in May Matthews' mind. The girl was uneasy. Her slender fingers worried a balled handkerchief from time to time. She darted quick glances in the direction of the card player as though assuring herself of his protection. She was tensed, nervous.

Couldn't blame her, thought Pat. She must figure him a killer. The day of the bushwhacking he had burst in upon them and told of shooting Dakota. May was a city girl, unaccustomed to violence. Was it surprising that she was scared?

After awhile, the constraint began to irk. He crushed his butt and rose. "I got to mosey along," he said, offhand.

"Back to town?" she inquired, with obvious relief.

"Maybe!" he returned vaguely. Her gray eyes weighed him, troubled. "You don't blame me," she questioned, "for riding into Adobe Wells and testifying?"

"Not one speck!" he assured her heartily. "The finger pointed straight at me — and you figure it still does!"

She gasped. "How can you say that, Pat?"

He smiled with bleak humor. "Heck, you act like you're scairt stiff."

Without replying, she swung away and stepped into the house.

In a sombre mood, he walked the gelding past the corral and set it to the slope beyond. It was plain he'd worn out his welcome at the Matthews' place. If Matt's killer wasn't caught, folks would always doubt his innocence. Like May, they'd never forget he'd followed the Circle heir away from the ranch, after a quarrel. The old-timers would have no doubt — Matt had hanged his father, he had beefed Matt! It was a logical sequence, another episode in the Harper-Bradley feud.

Not caring where he rode, he gave the

gelding its head. At a walk, it threaded through the tangle of upended terrain. Musing, its rider jerked the makin's out of his shirt pocket.

The gelding chose that moment to fiddle-foot nervously as a coiled rattlesnake raised its spade head on the trail ahead and rattled. The tobacco sack slipped from Pat's fingers. As he jerked downward, grabbing for the sack as it slid over the pony's smooth shoulder, a slug buzzed over his head and the whiplash of a Winchester crackled in his ears.

Without pause, he kicked free of the stirrups, threw himself sideways out of the saddle, came down on a shoulder and moved frantically over the ground seeking cover. Chips stung his face as another screaming bullet glanced off rock. He scrambled behind a boulder and lay panting. The gelding wandered on, carrying his own Winchester in the boot.

Bellied behind the sheltering boulder, Pat eyed the riderless pony. If he left cover to chase it, the unseen bushwhacker would likely cut him down before he'd taken a couple of paces.

If he remained, he was a sitting duck. Armed only with a short range Colt .45, he was helpless to return the fire. His only hope was that the Matthews would hear the shooting and investigate. Their appearance might scare the assassin off.

# XVIII

The sun climbed higher. A tiny whiptail lizard scuttled across the boulder, darted out of sight; a sidewinder slowly moved its looping length through littered rock, seeking cover. Pat resisted an impulse to plant a slug in the horned spade head. Maybe, he thought, that rattler had saved his life.

Pat eased his stained Stetson out beyond the flank of the boulder, as though he were cautiously peering. Couldbe it would draw fire. Nothing happened. A mothworn trick, he thought, yanking the Stetson on again. It wouldn't fool anyone but a greenhorn. But he was crazy to lie around, waiting to be shot like a setting hen.

Slowly, he began to ease backward, keeping the bulk of the boulder between his flattened form and the location from which he judged lead had spewed. Every nerve tautened at anticipation of the smashing impact of a slug. But as he eased over the canyon

185

floor, no lead droned in pursuit. Finally, he had moved so far beyond the boulder that it afforded no cover. In a surge of recklessness, he came to his feet. If the jasper hadn't pulled out, he decided, the lobo would have plugged him by now.

He swung around, striding awkwardly in his high-heeled riding boots, on the trail of his mount.

He found the gelding quietly nuzzling roots beyond an angle of the canyon. He gathered the trailing reins and swung into the saddle. Allowing the pony to drift ahead, he pondered on the bushwhack attempt — and the swarthy features of Jules Garrott became plain in his mind's eye. Who else would crave to down him except the Circle foreman? Garrott had made one attempt on his life outside the jail. He knew too much and was marked for elimination. Likely the breed had glimpsed him riding for the hills. It would have been easy to lay for him when he left the Matthews' place. He'd gamble Garrott had cut down Matt Bradley in exactly the same manner.

Cold anger began to build up inside the rider. Garrott had been back of most all the trouble that had plagued him since he had ridden into the Basin. It was long odds that if he didn't beef the breed, Garrott would surely get him. The showdown had been postponed too long. With sudden resolution, he raised the gelding to a canter. Before sundown, he determined, either he or the breed would qualify for boothill.

It was close upon noon when he rode into the rambling Circle B and reined down in the center of the yard. Perplexed, he sat eying punchers drifting aimlessly around, squatting on the top rail of the corral, hunkered against the bunkhouse wall. This was a weekday and the crew should have been out on the range, handling the many chores of a big spread. His head turned toward the house when the front door opened and Bones, followed by the rotund Doc Lockwood, stepped out.

Something was amiss, he thought, seriously amiss. He reined over to intercept them. The doctor sighted him and jerked to a stop. "Harper!" he exclaimed in astonishment. "I thought you were back in jail."

Pat ignored him. "What's wrong?" he asked the deputy shortly.

"Everything!" rasped the lawman.

"Such as?"

"Bull checked out sometime last night. Garrott and Diane are missing. There's a crazy story going around the crew that they rode out together afore sunup."

"Together!" ejaculated Pat.

"That's what I said," grated Bones.

"Diane hated the breed's guts."

"Wal, she left with the hairpin."

The doctor stood frowning at Pat. "Aren't you going to arrest this man?" he demanded.

"Nope!" snapped the deputy. "Pat's as clean as a hound's tooth." Without further explanation he turned and walked away. Shaking his head, the doctor followed.

His mind awhirl, Pat sat his pony. Diane — her father dead or dying — leaving with Garrott! It didn't make good sense. His thoughts went to when the girl had fought off the foreman's attack, and an explanation leapt into his mind. Garrott had abducted the girl. The notion seemed loco, but he could come up with no other answer.

Wasting no time conferring with the deputy, he raised his reins and headed south toward Coyote Butte.

Night enfolded the desert when the gelding's dragging hooves sank into talus heaped around the base of the Butte. Clifflike, the rugged flank of the rocky rampart rose high above. The waterhole, Pat knew, was on the further side, to the west.

He kneed the pony and it began to trudge

along the base of the rock, sinking even deeper into drifted talus. Its pace slowed; it faltered and suddenly, without warning, collapsed. Pat wrenched free and came to his feet. Sunk to the knees in feathery talus, he vainly endeavored to bring the spent animal to its feet.

Finally, he quit. The gelding was plainly played out. He unstrapped his spurs, slid the Winchester from its boot and plugged wearily ahead, afoot. A ragged jumble of sundered rock barred his way. Fighting cloying fatigue, he began scrambling and climbing up over the obstacle.

He reached the far side of the rockslide, thankfully found level ground beneath his feet — and no talus! Cautiously moving ahead, he rounded a shoulder of the Butte — and came to an abrupt stop. Not a hundred paces ahead, on the brink of a rock-cradled pool, a campfire glowed bright. Beside it sat Garrott, back propped against the curve of a saddle. Light from the leaping flames revealed the botched forms of two hobbled ponies amid sparse brush, beyond the pool. "Garrott!" breathed the rider. But where was Diane?

His searching eyes picked up a sleeping form, stretched on the far side of the fire. He caught the glint of firelight upon burnished hair and drew a deep breath of relief. Quietly he set the Winchester on the ground. He could have leveled on the foreman and cut him down with ease, but an itching urge possessed him to confront Garrott, face to face. He fingered the butt of his .45, eased the holster forward a mite, then began to walk forward, in no haste, his spurless boots silent on hard rock.

Step after step he advanced, eyes focused on Garrott, but the foreman, unconscious of the man stalking him in the starlight, placidly drew on a cornhusk cigarette. Within twenty paces of the fire now, Pat knew that the girl had awakened and sighted him. Her eyes, gleaming in the firelight, were fixed in an unwavering stare.

A loose rock clattered, displaced by one of his boots. Quick as a cat, the foreman was on his feet and whirling. He reached for his .45. Two guns spouted flame almost as one, the reports reverberating against the rock pile towering overhead.

# XIX

Garrott, his burly form silhouetted by the firelight, swayed, but his gun again stabbed fire. Throwing down for a second shot, Pat heard the drone of a slug. A knife seemed to stab into the calf of his right leg with numbing force. The leg buckled under him. He crashed down as the breed loosed a third shot. Frantically, the wounded rider rolled, striving to distract his opponent's aim and get outside the revealing circle of firelight.

Diane's anguished scream of dismay rang in his ears. Lead droned around him. He checked, sprawled on his belly, steadying the elbow of his gunarm on the bare rock — leveled on Garrott's dark silhouette. His gun spilled flame and thunder, once — twice. The foreman staggered, jerked upright, vainly striving to align his own gun. Then he slumped, limp as a wet sack. His smoking gun dropped from loosened fingers, hit rock with a metallic clank.

Peering through a fog of gunsmoke, Pat eyed the other's limp form. He tried to rise, but his right leg seemed useless. Slowly, he began to drag himself toward the fire. When he approached Garrott's heaped form, one glance at the sightless eyes staring at the starlit sky told him that the breed would make no more trouble in Big Basin.

Rounding the spluttering fire, he crawled to the side of Diane. "Oh Pat," she whispered, eyes big against the blur of her pale features, "I thought that brute had killed you." He saw that she was securely tied, legs bound together and hands lashed behind her.

"Seems I'm doggone hard to kill," he chuckled and, for no good reason, kissed her. The girl's lips met and clung to his.

He whipped out his jackknife and severed her lashings. With a deep sigh, she rose to a sitting position. He yanked the boot off his injured leg and sat wryly eying a ragged gash in the calf. "Guess I was lucky. Figured the bone was broken."

"It needs attention," she returned, "right now." Ripping a strip from her white underskirt, she bandaged the leg.

Pat pulled on his boot, levered to his feet. The leg seemed to carry his weight now. Limping to the fire, he dropped down by the saddle and leaned back thankfully against it. Now that the action was over, waves of fatigue seemed to flow through him. He felt tired, tuckered out, too tired to move, too tired to think. Nothing mattered now, he thought sleepily. Diane was safe; Garrott was dead.

The girl came over and sank down beside him, nestling close. Quite naturally, his arm went around her, gathering her close. "Wal," he inquired sleepily, "what happened back at the Circle?"

"A nightmare!" returned Diane tensely. "I was alone with Dad in the house. He's been unconscious for days. That — animal" — she nodded toward the foreman's limp body — "stole in. He grabbed me right in the bedroom, stuffed a filthy bandanna into my mouth and trussed me up. It was after midnight; no one else was around. He had those two saddle horses ready. He roped me to one and rushed me away." Her tremulous laugh told of ragged nerves. "It was as simple as that!"

"Just what was the idea?"

"Oh, he told me that, too. He — he intended taking me across the border, and giving me the option of being sold into a bawdy house or signing the Circle over to him." She began to weep silently.

"The skunk!" muttered Pat, and his circling arm tightened.

She clung to him. "Oh, Pat," she sobbed, "don't leave me — ever!"

"I sure won't," he promised softly, and again their lips met, hungrily.

Adobe Wells simmered in the heat of noon when Pat limped into the yellowed adobe that served as law shack. Bones was hunched at the plank table. His head came around at sound of the opening door and his flinty eyes focused the visitor. "Where you been hiding out?" he grated.

"Just been handling your chores while you set around like a broody hen," grinned the rider, and hooked up a chair.

"Spill it," grunted the deputy, "afore you bust."

"With pleasure," chuckled Pat and told of his ride to Coyote Wells and the fracas in which Garrott was killed.

Bones listened in silence, chewing the stem of his cold corncob. "Diane's at the hotel," concluded the rider. "We aim to get hitched."

"About time a wild young colt like you was broke to harness," growled the deputy.

"Guess that job that brought me back to the Basin's finished," continued Pat. "Matt's dead. Now Garrott's gone, the rustling gang'll likely break up. Reckon we'll have a spell of peace."

"So everything's hunky-dory!" commented Bones dryly. "You forgot that Matt's killer's on the loose?"

"Garrott plugged Matt. He craved to rod the gang."

Bones slowly shook his head. "Matt never rodded no gang. Garrott never beefed him. And we still got to put the finger on the boss rustler."

Pat stared, unbelieving. "You funning?"

"Funnin' — with a killer loose!" The deputy scraped back his chair. "Whatsay you and me take a walk."

"Where to?"

"The Matthews' place."

"What you figure to find there?"

"The bushwhack gun, mebbe."

"Now I know that what brains you got are scrambled," retorted Pat.

When the two riders jogged up to the weathered hill ranch, the T.B. victim was engrossed in solitaire. They dismounted and tied their ponies by the corral. Still wondering, Pat tailed the old deputy as Bones strode up to the gallery.

"Howdy!" he said, checking at the rail by

the card player.

The man glanced up, nodded briefly and returned to his cards.

"You keep any guns around here?" inquired the deputy.

"As you well know, we dislike firearms," snapped Judd Matthews. Pat saw the girl step out of the house and smiled at her reassuringly.

"I got a Winchester in mind," rambled on the deputy. "Mind if I poke around the house?"

With an impatient gesture, the invalid swept his cards aside. He swung around to face the old lawman. "I do mind," he barked. "What right have you to search my home? I am a sick man. I brought my daughter back into these hills in search of rest and quiet. We know nothing of Winchesters or Colts or any other brand of cannon. Go away and leave us in peace!"

"As a law abiding citizen, Mister Matthews," persisted Bones, unabashed, "you won't object if I peek into the house afore I leave."

"Peek — and be damned!" blazed Matthews.

The puzzled rider dogging him, Bones jingled toward the open door of the adobe. As they passed the girl, Pat eyed her sympathetically, mentally cursing Bones for a blundering old fool. May was plainly scared stiff at the intrusion.

He well remembered the interior of the adobe. There were two small rooms — bedroom and living room, with a lean-to built against the rear that served as kitchen. While Bones looked around, he stood eying the furnishings. There was the same old horsehair sofa, the scratched circular table, the pot bellied heating stove with its black lengths of pipe slanting ceilingward. He stepped to the bedroom door and glanced inside. Here the furnishings were new — a comfortable double bed, a shiny oak bureau, a conventional washstand with china pitcher and bowl, a woman's dressing table laden with bottles of perfume, jars of cream — a woman's doodads. His brow wrinkled as he glimpsed a man's shaving brush on the washstand, with a case of straight-edge razors.

*Kinda intimate,* he thought. *If they were father and daughter, why only one bed?*

The deputy brushed past him, yanked the coverings off the bed, investigated the mattress, dropped on his knees and peered underneath the bed. Then he moved to the closet, began fingering through suits and dresses hanging inside. Finally, with a

disgusted grunt, he joined Pat in the doorway and stood gnawing the ends of his
drooping mustache, plainly baffled.

"You upset things enough?" inquired the
rider. "I'd say you're acting plumb loco. The
Matthews wouldn't know the muzzle of a
gun from its butt."

But Bones' deepset eyes were probing the
living room again. Suddenly, he stepped
forward, grasped the slanted stovepipe and
wrenched. Soot showered as lengths of pipe
clattered down, breaking apart and clanking
over the floor.

Pat watched speechless, as the deputy
picked up one length after another, his left
arm black with soot as he investigated the
interior of each. His sooted hand came out
grasping a long object.

"Who's loco now?" rasped Bones and
strode to the door. Pat, behind him, saw
that May was standing beside the seated
form of her father, panic in her eyes. At the
doorway, the deputy levered a shell into the
breech, raised the barrel and pressed trigger. The gun whipcracked and bucked.
Bones ejected the spent shell, bent quickly
and picked it up. One glance and he handed
it to Pat. The metal hot on his fingers, the
rider eyed its base — the sharp indent of
the firing pin was off center, exactly as it

had been on the two bushwhack shells. This gun had killed Matt Bradley.

# XX

Bones' right arm, blurring for his hand gun, knocked the brass case out of Pat's hand. Startled, the rider's head jerked up, to see Judd Matthews standing half-crouched by the card table, a snub-nosed derringer clutched in his fist. The squat derringer spat crimson and the astounded Pat heard the plonk of the bullet as it bedded in an upright supporting the gallery behind him. Then the roar of Bones' long-barrelled Colt thundered in his ears.

The heavy slug plowed into Matthews' chest, smashed him backward. Already dead, he flopped across the card table. It turned over. Playing cards showered the corpse as it thudded down. Screaming hysterically, the girl threw herself upon the inert form.

"I'll — be — damned!" gasped Pat.

Bones dropped his gun back into the holster and strode down the gallery toward the girl bent sobbing over Matthews' bloodied remains.

"You crave to ride to town, ma'am?" he inquired unemotionally.

"Not with you, you dirty killer!" she shrilled. "Judd was a better man than you, than any one of you." Smooth features contorted with fury, she lunged for the derringer, lying beside the upturned table.

The deputy's long leg swung. He booted the weapon out of her reach. "Gimme a hand with the body," he directed over a shoulder. "Guess we'll pack it back with us." Pat hastened forward.

Shades of oncoming night slowly erased the hills as the deputy and Pat jogged toward Adobe Wells. Behind the lawman, Judd Matthews' remains were roped over a led pony. Shock of the discovery of the .44 Winchester and the invalid's swift demise kept Pat silent. Finally, he voiced the question that drummed in his brain. "How in creation did you know that the Matthews' had that Winchester cached?"

Bones' dry chuckle was that of a thoroughly satisfied man. "Wal," he confessed, "I played a hunch. It's a long story."

"And you're itching to tell it, you old crow," retorted the rider. "I'm listening with both ears."

The deputy brought out his corncob pipe, tapped it on the saddlehorn, stuffed tobacco into the bowl. "I first got a notion this Matthews hombre was running some sort of a blazer when I dropped in, checking on Matt's killing," he confessed. "While he's stating that guns is something about which he knows less than nothing, a hideaway is bulging his coat below the left armpit. He was right slick with the paste-boards, too — handled 'em like a professional gambler. It struck me he was maybe on the lam, hiding out. So I forward his description to the sheriff at Bonita and inquire if they got anything in the files." He spat. "There was plenty!"

"Seems the gent we're packing to town was known as Diamond Dan Hartman. He ran a poker game in the Eldorado Saloon, Tombstone, Arizona Territory. A cowman caught him four-flushing. He drilled the hombre, ripped up another gent who horned in from bellybutton to brisket, and lit out."

"His daughter's no saloon floosy!" threw in Pat defensively.

"Daughter, hell!" snorted Bones. "That skirt was a dancer in the Eldorado. She beat it with him."

"Not May!"

"Gawd!" groaned the deputy. "It don't take more'n a pretty face and calf's eyes to fool some soft-hearted mavericks. In Arizona she was Dolores Delacorte, and she danced stark naked.

"Wal, Hartman and the skirt switch monikers and drift into Adobe, hunting a spot to hole up. They make a deal with your paw and move into the hills. But Hartman don't crave the old man around, seeing he's already working in cahoots with Jules Garrott, organizing a rustling gang to bleed the cowmen white. So Garrott slaps your paw's brand on a bunch of Circle steers and toles Matt onto 'em. You know Matt, hotheaded — he swings your paw.

"Then you turn up and you're too damned nosy to suit Hartman. Guess you went soft on the gal and run off too much at the mouth." Pat remembered revealing to May his double role and squirmed inwardly. The old deputy droned on. "So Hartman decides to plant you beside your paw. He has Garrott send you south with a rustled herd, and tips me off — remember the anonymous note? — figuring you'll stop a slug or draw a long term in the pen when I pick you up at Coyote Wells. But Dakota, the herd boss, had a pard name of Hawkins. Hawkins joins my posse and ruins the play, with an 'accidental' gunshot.

"After your near-hanging I pick up Hawkins and give him a choice — face charges of rustling and attempted murder, or spill the beans. He spilled the beans, aplenty."

Bones' weathered features crinkled as he chuckled dryly. "Reckon you gave Hartman a shock when you rode in after downing Dakota in the hideaway. He figured you dead or a prisoner. The lobo was a fast thinker. You tangle with Matt; Matt's a pest, hanging around the gal. So, when you pull out on Matt's trail, he grabs his Winchester and lays for Matt. Then he sends the skirt to town to report a bushwhacking. The finger points straight at you, as he figured it would." The deputy's voice held respectful homage. "A perfect frameup!"

"Then Hartman thinks some more. Maybe you'll talk in court, incriminate Garrott and wreck the rustling set up. So he arranges the jail break."

"The lousy, double-crossing sidewinder," muttered Pat. "And dying of T.B. at that."

"Dying, hell!" threw back Bones. "That T.B. was arrested years back. Hartman was as healthy as a hog." Amusement in his deepset eyes, he turned in the saddle and surveyed his companion. "Wal, everything plain?"

"Plain as the ears on a jackass," admitted Pat. "And I've a notion I'm the jackass."